Ordinary Snowflakes

A Rock Creek Christmas Novella

ISBN: 978-0-9978508-1-9

Ordinary Snowflakes

Printed in the United States of America
First Printing, 2016
Edited by Dori Harrell of Breakout Editing

Cover Design by Jennifer Rodewald and
Roseanna White of www.RoseannaWhiteDesigns.com
Images from www.Shutterstock.com

Published by Rooted Publishing
McCook, NE 69001

Ordinary Snowflakes

Jennifer Rodewald

*You will find a baby wrapped in cloths
and lying in a manger.*

~Luke 2:12~

Chapter One

I almost stepped on it.

A small brown box with a simple strip of burlap around it lay conspicuously on my tiny front porch. Like a wordless little message.

I see you.

My heart quivered a little bit as I knelt to scoop the brown-papered mystery. It would have looked shabby-chic, except for the strip holding it together had been tied in a knot—and not even a fancy one. Still, it was a gift, probably.

Standing, my breath hitched as I paused on my porch. When I exhaled, the warm, moist air left my mouth in puffs of white. I surveyed the quiet neighborhood beyond my short drive. Crisp, sparkling frost dressed the tree-lined street with winter's finest, making me shiver.

Oh for a beach, a warm breeze, and the sun on my bare skin.

Three doors down, a car steamed its filmy exhaust into the frosty air in a neighbor's drive. Wished I'd thought of warming up my vehicle too. Or had the time.

I glanced down at the box again. The longing for a summer escape fizzled. *Someone noticed me.* Maybe winter wasn't all that bad...

"Mom!" Sydney pushed against the back of my legs. "We're gonna be late. Let's go!"

Late was standard in our world. Didn't usually bother my seven-year-old daughter. But today...we couldn't be late today, heaven bless it. Today was the snowflake party at school, and Mr. Somebody Special I hadn't met yet was coming to sing winter-wonderland songs.

"He's so great, Mom," Sydney had said when this mystical child charmer had made his first entry into her young life. "He helped us make leaf tapestries, and we sang about the colors of fall and pumpkins and everything amazing about autumn."

Gushy. My daughter was gushy about this guy, and had been for the past three months.

Probably because she longed for that kind of man in her real, everyday life.

Yeah, me too. But I was the do-it-all mom, so I keep it real.

"Slow down, Princess Hurry Up, or you'll fall," I called after the pink-parka-with-pigtails rushing down the steps. "There's ice on that walk, and I didn't shovel the drive."

Sydney made it to the corner without wiping out and stopped. She spun around and scowled at me. "Are you losing it? The driveway's clear." She grinned, shaking her head. "Maybe you need more coffee. Good thing you're a baroness."

"Barista, silly. I'm a barista." A chuckle left my mouth. "A baroness is an important lady someplace far away. I serve coffee."

"That's important."

For some of us, it was essential. I grinned as I caught up to her, tugging on the raven ponytail closest to me. "Whatever we do..."

"We do it for Him." One little, surprisingly clean finger pointed toward the heavily clouded sky.

"That's right." I gripped the hand that still stretched over her head. "So let's get to it."

Coming round the corner, the cleared drive finally sank into my understanding. Sydney may have been right—I was losing it. But I would have sworn on her birthday that I hadn't scooped the snow. I'd overslept and barely had time to get her and me ready, squeezing a half a cup of java in somewhere in the madness.

I hadn't scooped the snow. I knew I hadn't.

After opening the car door, I slid into the driver's seat and looked at the small mystery package that I'd stuffed into my purse.

What on earth...

"Mom-ster, go! He'll be there already, and I can't wait."

Snowflake party day. Almost as fun as Christmas, just two weeks away.

I bit my bottom lip, tucking a grin beneath my teeth. I learned five years ago not to invest too much emotion in daydreams. Reality was just a bit too harsh to risk the cost. But what if...

The pregnant sky overhead began drifting in white specks to the ground, slowly, like a pail of cotton tipping on its side. Flakes of snow dusted my windshield, and for a moment I let wonder take me captive. Tiny gems of solid water glistened like jewels across my vision, and it seemed like possibilities drifted down with their silent beauty.

For me, this was a rare moment of appreciation for winter.

Someone had noticed me. A secret admirer? A man with a good heart, who saw how much I actually did need help, even though I never admitted it, and how much Sydney needed someone to teach her that men could be nice—that some of them stuck around, no matter how hard life got. Maybe I knew him. Maybe he'd been around for a while. Maybe this was the beginning of a beautiful story—a romance full of hope and second chances and love. Maybe...

Not gushy at all, right? *Way to keep it real.*

Snowflakes continued to drift around my cold car. Wonder diminished. They were just ordinary snowflakes falling on my ordinary life.

I tucked the package deeper into my purse and started the car, clearing the snow from my windshield, and the maybes from my imagination. Out of sight, out of mind, I hoped.

***

"So what's in it?" Jane leaned over my shoulder, peering at the brown box in my purse.

"I don't know."

"Kale." She straightened, poking a hand on one hip. "You didn't open it?"

I snapped my bag shut. Curiosity was killing me, but maybe it was some dumb car part sent to the wrong address, or something equally crushing. How was I going to swallow that kind of disappointment?

A car part mailed without a label and an attempt at gift-like wrapping? Made perfect sense.

"Give me that." Jane moved to snatch the purse I'd just tucked into my employee cubby.

I stepped in between her and my mystery gift. "No. You can't. We have to work."

"I won't remember orders or how to make a latte or anything useful if we don't look." Jane's eyes melted into a puppy plea. "Come on, Kale. It's killing me. I don't know how it's not *killing* you. We have to look."

"What are you two girls doing back here, all huddled together like a pair of high schoolers?" Ms. Ruthie stood at the backroom doorway, her arms crossed, desperately trying to pull off stern. She couldn't. Nice went all the way through my generous employer, like sweet went through a solid-chocolate Santa.

I grinned at Jane and then at Ms. Ruthie. "Nothing. We were just coming. Is it busy?"

"Joe just walked in. Don't expect much of anyone else with the weather."

"I'll get his hot chocolate." I set a look on Jane. "Don't touch it. I mean it."

Jane let her shoulders droop as if I'd just killed Christmas.

Ruthie looked between the two of us and caught my arm before I squeezed through the door. "What's this?"

"Kale has a secret admirer. Left a gift at her door and shoveled her driveway clear this morning."

Ms. Ruthie's eyes lit up. "What was the gift?"

"She hasn't opened it."

"And I'm not going to right now." I wiggled out of Ms. Ruthie's light hold. "I have work to do."

"Mmm-m." Ms. Ruthie hummed behind me. "Christmas is a good time to fall in love."

And that made two against me. They should know better—they'd been around during that dark time when my world fell apart. Sydney's accident was too much for her father, and the fact that we weren't married made leaving an easy answer. For him. I couldn't go back there again—depending on a man only to be left alone with all the hard stuff. It was better if I knew up front it was all on me.

Better if I just kept it real. And reality said that if I intended to get Sydney the Princess Lego Palace she'd set her heart on for Christmas, I'd better work extra hard for those tips. That didn't leave room for daydreams about secret admirers.

I finished tying my crisp white apron around my waist as I approached the counter and the only customer in the coffeehouse. "Morning, Joe. Hot chocolate this morning?"

"I'm so predictable, aren't I?"

"We'll call it reliable." I grinned, reaching for the soup-bowl-sized mug we gave to our regulars. "You want whip?"

"You have to ask?"

I chuckled. Indeed, Joe was reliable. Large hot chocolate, extra whip, no sprinkles. Hot in the winter, chilled in the summer. Never failed.

Steam drifted from the spout as I poured his cocoa, the

heavenly smell of milk chocolate making my stomach growl. "Where are you today?"

Joe White's job was a little unconventional. Not his job, actually, but the way he went about it. The only physical therapist in a town that didn't even have a doctor's clinic, he didn't have an office in the common sense. Home visits. Appointments at the school and at the nursing home. High school athletic events. I wasn't sure how he kept up with it all, but as far as I knew, he'd never failed anyone. Mr. Reliable indeed.

"The school. Mr. Erikson is coming, and he has some special activities planned, so they asked me to be there for my younger patients."

"Mr. Erikson..." I squirted a healthy dollop of whip on the top of his full mug and handed it across the counter. "Is that the man my daughter has been raving about?"

Joe chuckled. "Probably. He's a kid charmer. Think Mr. Rogers meets Tim Tebow, and you've got our Mr. Craig Erikson. He sings, he's silly, and he's got those kids enraptured. Today is the snowflake party, and I'm sure he'll make it amazing."

I leaned a hip on the counter. "Where'd he come from?"

Joe shrugged. "Don't know. All I know is he travels around the regional schools, bringing delight wherever he goes." A long pause extended, and Joe's expression changed as if something just hit him. "Gotta run." He turned away, blowing on his drink.

"Wait, run?" Mr. Predictable just threw a curveball. He

usually sat near the middle window, opened his Bible and his copy of *Our Daily Bread*, and sipped his cocoa while reading.

"Yeah. Like I said, I'm at the school today, so…"

"Do you want a to-go cup?"

He looked at the giant ceramic mug in his hand. "Oh. Uh…" Then one long drink later—which had to burn—he set the mug back on the counter and spun away. "Sorry. Not thinking straight today. Don't worry about it."

Gone. The man trekked out of the coffeehouse with three long strides, not even glancing back.

Weird. But I guessed that was how the day was gonna go. Reaching for his abandoned drink, I glanced around the vacant room. I'd have to dump it anyway—one sip wasn't going to hurt.

Sweet chocolate warmed my tongue and then my belly. Pretty good. Considering I was a coffee girl, this was a strange move for me.

But like I said, that was how the day was gonna go. I might as well roll with it.

***

Slow days were the worst. Not only were tips a sad handful of a few bills and coins, but time dragged out like a snail on a dirt road. Which left plenty of room to wonder what was in that brown package still tucked in my purse. And about this mysterious Mr. Erikson, child superhero and apparently man extraordinaire.

Jane finished wiping the tables for the third time and approached me at the counter, where I was disposing coffee grounds. "What'd you say to Joe this morning?"

I straightened from my hunched position over the

trash. "Huh?"

"Joe White. He took off. What'd you say to him?"

"Nothing."

Her eyebrows curved in. "Nothing? Why'd he leave?"

"Said he had to go. I don't know." I finished tugging the garbage bag out and tied it off. "Why?"

"Just thought you mentioned the mystery gift."

"Why would I do that? And why would that send him out the door?"

A sly grin and a lifted brow transformed Jane's face. "Because maybe he's the giver."

I couldn't stop the laugh that bubbled from my chest. "Joe? Jane, you've been reading too many novels. I've known the guy for five years. He's my daughter's physical therapist. We go to the same church. I see him here every day. If he'd been interested in me, he'd have said something a long time ago. We're just friends."

"He's kind of cute."

Joe, with his dark hair and ready grin, was more than cute. Cute was for puppies. Joe was handsome, and any girl with eyeballs could see that. But frankly, even if he was the giver, there was no chemistry between him and me. Not like there had been with Brad. With Brad...oh my. The first time I saw that man, my knees actually buckled. Tall, dark, and swoony, that guy.

Guess he knew it too. But he set his sights on me, which didn't make a whole lot of sense. I was just an average girl. Nothing runway worthy about my straight brown tresses, ordinary face, and eyes the same color as my hair. So when he pursued me and the chemistry kept charging ahead...well, logic and boundaries took a backseat. Suddenly I was pregnant. And then a mom. And then after Sydney's injuries proved to be more complicated than broken bones, Mr. Swoony took off, claiming he wasn't made for these kinds of burdens.

Apparently I was. Knuckle down and love hard. That was how Sydney and I made it the past few years. With a lot of help from my parents. And Joe.

I had yet to have my knees buckle around another man—Joe White included. Which likely meant my romance days were behind me—and that was probably for the best.

Chapter Two

I pulled up to Rock Creek Elementary School a little before three, which was noteworthy, as I was never early. For anything. But an empty coffee shop and a growing concern for a pending blizzard sent me off work early. Like I said, it was a weird day.

Squealing children beckoned me from the back of the school, and when I stepped into the front office to check in, the secretary directed me out to the playground around back.

"The kindergartners are finishing their snowflake party on the hill," she said.

"The hill?"

"Yes." Mrs. Anderson grinned. "Mr. Erikson brought sleds."

I gripped the counter and leaned toward the senseless woman. "Sleds?"

She missed my tone of *strong* disapproval, instead setting a gleaming look on me. "He's dreamy, that Mr. Erikson. Have you met him?"

"No." I didn't change my cold tone.

She wiggled her eyebrows. "He'd be quite a catch..."

Oh, he was gonna catch something all right. I

snatched the visitor's badge she'd passed toward me and spun out of the door. Double-timing my way around back, I caught my first glimpse of the hill as I raced around the corner of the school building. Near panic had my heart thundering as I scanned the white blanketed hill for a dark-haired girl in a pink camo parka.

And then I found her. Not at the bottom, making snow angels and being safe.

My daughter squirmed her way onto a disk sled with *Joe White* standing behind her, ready to give her a hearty shove down the hill. *Joe.* Her physical therapist. The man who'd seen her crushed legs after they came out of a cast when she was two years old. The man who'd became a consistent part of our world after we spent two weeks in a Denver hospital for bone grafts. The man who had walked with us through the agonizing process of constant therapy—dreadful, painful therapy, not to mention several more surgeries—to get us to the point where she could finally wear braces at the age of three and learn to walk again.

What in South America was Joe thinking?

My legs went on marching autopilot until I reached a tall, well-built man at the bottom of the hill.

"Nice crash, Sydney!" the idiot yelled.

My heart stalled, and nausea pushed into my throat as I watched my special-needs daughter roll off the disk and tumble head over heels twice before she finally stopped in a rumpled heap in the snow. She lay still for two heartbeats, and I moved to rush after her. As my jog broke into an all-out run, she sat up, threw her hands above her head, and laughed.

"That was a ten!" she shouted. "So a ten! Right, Joe?"

"Totally a ten," idiot man behind me hollered.

I spun a one-eighty and stomped toward him. "What on earth are you thinking?" I snatched the man's elbow and ripped him around to face me. "Do you know what could have happened? That kid—*my* kid—walks with a pair of braces strapped to her legs. One wrong fall and—"

"Whoa." Mr. Irresponsible threw up both hands and stepped back. "Easy there, mama bear. I cleared it with Joe. He's been with her the whole time."

I stepped forward, eliminating the personal space he'd just put between us. "Joe? Joe White is *not* Sydney's parent!"

A hand to my elbow interrupted my righteous attack. "Kale, come on."

I spun around. Right into Joe, said permission giver, and thus the real target of my anger. With a hand to his parka-cushioned chest, I pushed him. "What are you thinking? Sydney? On a sled? Do you really think I can handle another emergency room visit? Do you have any idea how much an ambulance costs?"

"Calm down, Kale." Joe's hand, which had somehow managed to stay anchored on my elbow, slid up and squeezed my shoulder. "Syd is fine. She's just fine, and I wouldn't put her in any real danger."

I glared at him for a full three seconds. The last time I'd been this furious with a man...

"Mrs. Brennan." The big man behind me spoke again.

"Miss." I flung the correction over my shoulder and then sidestepped Joe, who still stood with a scowl. Raising my voice so my daughter could hear me, I summoned her as I moved away from both men. "Sydney, it's time to go."

"Mom! Come on. One more go?"

"No." I kept moving toward the parking lot around the front of the school. "Home. Now."

"Aw, man."

Common reaction. Someday I probably should teach her to say *yes, ma'am*, or something equally impressive. If I ever find the time and energy to do that superparent trick.

I didn't wait. I was too mad to look at Joe and too scared to look back at the hill. All I'd see would be my daughter tumbling to a pink-camo splat at the bottom. That'd be awesome. One wrong break, and she'd lose a leg.

One wrong break! Joe—

My blood ran hot and my ears burned. He knew better.

"Thank you, Mr. Erikson. See ya, Joe!"

By the sound of her voice, Sydney trailed behind me. I drew a gulp of cold winter air, desperate for it to chill my temper. By the time I reached my car, my heart rate was nearly normal, and I was almost able to set aside the disaster I'd constructed in my head.

"Ms. Brennan."

I hadn't expected the stranger to follow me. Rolling my shoulders back, I turned to face him, stiff, because all the mad hadn't gone out of me yet. "What?"

"I'm sorry. I thought Joe was able to make that call. I didn't know."

A sigh sagged through my chest. How could the man have known the extent of Sydney's issues? She walked with a hitch in her gait, and her run looked like young Forest Gump, but really, what was a traveling elementary music teacher going to know about all of it?

"I know. I shouldn't have yelled at you. It wasn't your fault."

Sydney caught up to us, a grin still frozen on her innocent face. If only she could enjoy life like this...

"Great day today, Syd." He held a gloved palm out to her.

She smacked it with her mitted hand and giggled. "Yeah. When are you coming back?"

"Next week, and I've got a break, so I'll be around the whole time. Sound good?"

"Awesome!" Sydney fist pumped the air and hopped into the back of our Taurus.

I shut the door behind her, and he bent over to wave.

The man straightened from his hunched-over position and studied me for a breath. A small grin played on his mouth, making his blue eyes sparkle. "I think this was a bad introduction. Can I try again?"

Oh goodness, he smiled for real. My knee joints turned to Jell-O, and I thought, *Please. Let's have a do-over.*

"I'm Craig Erikson."

Easy there, oh teenaged version of my adult self. Let's not swoon. I extended my hand to his waiting one. "Kale Brennan."

He held our handshake for two more breaths after we actually shook. I didn't move. What girl would, with blue eyes smiling down on her and warm strength wrapped around her knuckles? But silently gawking was juvenile.

"Sydney has talked of you almost nonstop."

He ducked, as if my implied compliment embarrassed him.

Jell-O knees wobbled.

"She's a sweet girl. I've enjoyed getting to know her."

I'd enjoy getting to know you too. Despite my swoony thoughts, I was actually a grown up, I promise. Just my girly-twitter self managed to slip past my single-mom self.

And oh, I so hoped I hadn't said that out loud. Surely I didn't. I couldn't have.

Snowflakes began to drift around us, melting against my burning cheeks and reminding me that the winter storm warning was still in effect and I should go to the grocery store before it shut down.

"She's a good kid, and I'm a little overprotective sometimes."

Wasn't that a nice recovery? Totally adult, and humble besides.

"Understandable. Again, I apologize." He paused, leaned back as if an invisible string was tugging him away but he didn't want to go.

Wished I could cut that invisible thing.

"Listen, I've got to finish up class here. Mrs. Day left me in charge for the rest of the afternoon. But maybe I'll see you around next week?"

Oh, definitely. Small town. Big, handsome kid-charming man. Shouldn't be too hard to spot.

"I work over at the Java Palace."

Nice job, Kale. How about a sign? *Single mom works at coffee shop. You have been warned.* That should put an end to this.

Prince Charming nodded, smile still firmly in place. "I'll be sure to find you then, Ms. Kale Brennan. Like I said, I'll be around all week."

Be still my crazy palpitating heart.

And then he winked.

I died. Right up until Joe White strode my way, passing my fairy-dream-man hero with a nod and what I assume was some kind of man pleasantry. *Later, dude.* Something like that.

No, Mr. Craig Erikson would not say *dude.* I was certain.

"Kale, wait up."

Jell-O knees became flesh and bone, and the anger that had cooled into moldable clay became smoldering lava again.

"I don't think you want to talk to me right now, Joe."

He jogged the remaining fifteen feet. "Listen. I had it under control. I know what I'm doing, and you need to trust me."

I folded my arms across my chest. "She's not your kid, and up until you pulled that sled stunt, I did trust you."

"She's stronger than you think, and you need to let her be a kid." He took another step toward me. "She's got to learn how to take calculated risks, or she's going to be a bubble child the rest of her life."

"She is *not* a bubble child! And I don't think you get to make that call." I inched toward him, my vision locked on his. Why did he think he got to be mad? "You don't know—"

"I've been with you since the accident, Kale. I do know. She's seven years old, and she can barely run. She can't jump. Can't skip. Never gets to play tag with the other kids on the playground." Somehow he'd inched my way, or I his, until the white puff of his breath dusted my nose. "Is this how you want her to live?"

I ignored the sweet scent of cinnamon on his breath. "I want her in one piece."

He stared, fire and some kind of something else I couldn't define smoldering in his eyes, and then stepped back. After he glanced at the ground, he rubbed the back of his neck. "I know you do." His tone had softened, and he looked back at me, sadness in his expression. "I'm sorry."

I should have let it go. After all, Sydney was fine. But this...what was it? An overstep? Where did Joe get off making that kind of a decision for me? And accusing me of bubble wrapping my daughter?

Mad kept boiling. I huffed, still glaring at him, until he looked back at me.

He said nothing. Just held momentary eye contact and then glanced over his shoulder, back at the activity still happening on the hill. When his attention returned, he'd gone back to Joe, my daughter's physical therapist. Not Joe, the interfering guy who'd just made my blood simmer.

"So now you've met the famous Craig Erikson."

A tiny grin tickled my mouth. "I have."

He blinked but didn't look away. "Nice guy."

"He is—seems so."

Joe nodded and then looked past me into the back

window of my car. He moved, one hand touching my shoulder as he leaned around me to reach eye level with Sydney. She pressed her nose against the window and smiled.

With an index finger, he pushed against the glass where her nose squished. "See you, kiddo."

Sydney grinned, leaned back, and matched his index finger with one of her own. "Not if I see you first," she hollered through the glass.

Joe straightened, gave me one last silent look, and then stepped away.

"Bye, Kale. Be safe."

My heart somehow hurt. It didn't make any sense.

Chapter Three

My phone woke me up at 5:45. a.m., people. That was just wrong. And the worst—it was because the school was calling me, letting me know that students were not to come in because of the continuing blizzard. Snow day. Appropriate, following their snowflake party, *but 5:45 in the morning?* Very funny.

I snoozed for another hour, the back of my brain packing coloring books and puzzles and snacks for my daughter to take to work, because this mama had to earn some money. Christmas was coming. Though I knew Ms. Ruthie wasn't going to mind, I fought the ever-present mom guilt that I wore close to my heart. You know, the little dark voice always saying things like, *You didn't play with her enough today*, or *You disciplined when you should have given grace*, or *You coddled her when you should have disciplined*, or *You haven't given her enough fruits and vegetables, and for goodness sake, it's maybe time to start reading food labels. What if all the eat-real people are right and I'm poisoning my kid with blue-box pasta?* Or my personal favorite: *Connor's and Julia's and Allison's moms don't work. They stay home and raise their kids.* That one never faded.

And I wondered why I didn't sleep well.

That morning the ever-growing list of guilty bullet

points included the new one I went to bed with last night— *You shouldn't have ripped into Joe like that*, and a fresh *What kind of mom takes her kid to work with her?*

It was bound to be a great day.

With a long, exaggerated breath out, I made up my mind to get up and face it. As I sat up and put my feet on the floor, my phone rang again.

"Y-ello?" I yawned, and didn't bother to cover it. Whoever was calling at this still-dark hour deserved the subtle guilt trip. Call it sharing the wealth.

"Up and at 'em, eh, Kale?" Jane's despicable morning-person voice mocked me.

I didn't laugh. "Why are you calling me? Don't you know the rule?"

"Not before eight." She laughed. "Except today. Don't come in. The roads are bad, and the wind is howling. I'm here, but I doubt anyone will come in today, and Ruthie says you should stay home with Syd."

I flopped back against the mattress. A day off...should have made me happy. But how was I ever going to save for that Lego thing now? I didn't have sick days, PTO, or anything like that. I couldn't afford a no-pay playdate with my daughter, no matter how badly we could use it.

"Kale?"

"Yeah. I hear you. Okay." I pulled the phone from my ear.

"Kale, are you okay?"

"Dandy." I tried, unsuccessfully, to smother my

annoyance. "I'll see you Monday."

"Don't be like that. What's wrong?"

I swallowed, a burn suddenly stinging my eyes. I didn't cry, especially about something as dumb as a snow day, so I sat up and lifted my chin. "Nothing, Jane. I just need some coffee. Stay safe out there, and call me if anything interesting happens, okay?"

"Okaaay..."

That was going somewhere, and I needed to snuff it. "Great. Bye."

It was generally rude to just hang up when you knew the other person wasn't really prepared. I didn't stand on ceremony though, so that was what I did. Now, to get the day started.

Having stopped at the store the afternoon before, I had on hand eggs and the fixings for homemade hot chocolate. Sydney would wake up to a hot breakfast— which was not normal in our house—and a sweet treat. The thought of her joy lifted my grumpiness. That and the smell of the brew I'd started.

A snow day might be good. We could make snow angels—pending the wind ceasing. *Please, God?* And we could walk down to my parents' later this afternoon. I needed to check on Dad anyway, and we'd be able to have a long visit. If Dad was lucid enough, he'd play Skip-Bo with Sydney. That'd make it a ten for my little girl, which would totally redeem my skid-start morning.

I settled my plan as I whisked cocoa and sugar together before adding them to the milk. The heat under the pot began to work its magic, releasing that warm, inviting smell of milk chocolate throughout my small kitchen.

Made me think of Joe.

I should call and apologize. Except, then he'd think he'd have leave to do something like that again. I wasn't ready for that.

Could Sydney really not skip?

Another guilt bullet point to add to the lineup for the coming night—*First of all, how can you be a good mother and not know whether or not your kid can skip? And second, she can't skip?*

Excellent relaxation thoughts.

I pushed pause on the spiraling trend happening in my head. This was going to be a good day. I was going to make it be a good day.

"What's that yummy smell, Mom?"

Princess Sleepyhead came hobbling down the short hall to our kitchen, one fist rubbing at the sleep in her eye and the other clutching the satin-edged fleece blanket my mom had sewn for her when she was in the hospital.

She looked like a sweet little doll. Who cared if she could skip?

"Hot cocoa, and the eggs will be ready in just a few minutes."

"Is it Christmas?"

Down, guilt—it didn't matter if my daughter only thought I made real breakfast on Christmas. "Nope. Snow day."

Sleep instantly evaporated from her little body. "Snow day! Are you serious?"

"Yep."

Blankie took a flight through the house as Sydney trotted with her awkward gait through every available path. "Woo-hoo!"

She could too run, Joe White. Barely. That was what he'd said. She could barely run. Given her injuries, that was to be expected. What had he been thinking? Like he would know better.

He was only a physical therapist.

Good grief. I needed to just call him and apologize so he'd get out of my head.

The scrambled eggs solidified, and I sprinkled cheese over them while they were still in the pan. The shreds melted into tempting pools of orange and white, and I scooped a healthy portion onto a plate.

"Breakfast, Princess." I slid her dish onto the table and moved to pour her a small mug of cocoa. Once she was settled, Sydney reached for my hand, and we bowed together.

"Can I pray, Mom-ster?"

"Sure."

"Jesus, thank you for snow and hot chocolate and eggs and no school. For Your glory, amen."

No school for God's glory. Not sure how that worked, but I was sure He could find a way.

Sydney didn't waste any time worrying about it, instead shoveling a forkful of eggs into her mouth.

"Can we play Life?"

"Your mouth is full."

She groaned, tipped her head back and forth while she chewed faster, and then swallowed. "Can we?"

"Sure. But I need to make a phone call. Sit still and don't choke, 'kay?"

"Yep."

I pushed away from the table, my mug of coffee in hand, and snatched my phone from the counter. Once I'd reached my room, I pushed my door until only a crack existed between it and the doorjamb.

So secretive. Surely it'd be good for my daughter to hear me apologize for being rude. Kids needed a model, right? I reached for the knob, but my hand just stayed there, doing nothing.

What was I going to say to him? *Sorry I came unglued, but don't ever do that again?* To which he'd reply, *That's okay, but you're wrong. She needs it.*

Plus, we were friends. It'd blow over. What was he going to do, ignore me because I got upset? Not Joe. Wasn't the first time we'd clashed. He'd thought Sydney was ready for leg braces when she turned three. I didn't. We argued. Syd got leg braces two months after. Was that his win or mine? He thought I didn't need to hold her back from kindergarten a full year—she was smart and social and determined. I most certainly disagreed—she was small, and she needed a little more protection than most, and she'd spent her toddler years in and out of hospitals.

Syd started school two months before she turned seven. My win.

Except, during math time, she was bored because she was beyond the group. And she'd be nineteen when she graduated high school. Sigh. What was I thinking?

That she wasn't ready. Or I wasn't ready.

I should apologize to him. He was probably right. Maybe.

Later. He likely wasn't even up. The whole town was buried under snow, after all. Who would need a physical therapist in a blizzard?

Later. That would be a much better plan.

"Mom, I'm done. I'm getting out the game!"

See? I was busy anyway. Playing the game of Life. That was going to be interesting. I stunk at the real version.

***

The wind died down a little before eleven that morning. Good thing, because Life was killing me. Snow continued to fall, but instead of blinding the view beyond my window, the fluffy ice crystals drifted happily down to the waiting blanket of buddy flakes. Must be the more friendly side of the family.

The thought of family poked at my earlier decision to check on my parents. Syd and I could walk—the streets were still a mess—but I'd pack a basket to take with us. We'd do lunch.

"I'm getting my snow pants." Sydney's declaration came from her bedroom. "Come on, Mom-ster. It's snow angel time."

Okay. First snow angels. I sent a quick text to my mom to let her know we'd be over later and not to make lunch, and then tugged on my winter garb. By the time we were ready to fling ourselves into the drifts, we looked like colorful versions of the Michelin Man topped with puff-ball crocheted stocking hats.

Sydney charged out the door ahead of me, and I watched as she kicked her legs out to the side in her attempt to run.

She couldn't run. Not really. I thought that was to be expected, considering. But Joe...

I really should call him.

But not right then. Snow angels with Syd.

"This one's perfect. Line it up, Mom-ster."

I hadn't told her yet not to call me that. Sounded too much like monster, but she was so cute when she was excited. And I liked that we could sometimes be buddies, that she didn't always think of me as her half-baked, crazy-tired, usually crabby mother.

"All right, Syd-rome. Am I counting, or are you?"

"Both. We go on three. One..."

I joined the countdown. "Two..."

Simultaneously, we stuck our arms out parallel to the ground. "Three!"

I fell back, landing with a whoosh in the three-foot drift of fresh snow. Sydney stayed on her feet. The stinker.

"Game change." She grinned, turning to face me. "Dog pile!"

Before I could put my arms up to catch her, Sydney leaped forward, landing crossways on my stomach.

Oh my goodness, she was bigger than I thought. I grunted, dropping my head back into the snow. "Not fair. You blindsided me."

"Did you just tackle your mom, Sydney Brennan?"

Sydney wiggled, pushed her hands against my coat, and struggled to her feet. "Mr. Erikson!"

Oh no. Mr. Make-My-Knees-Mushy Erikson was

calling to my daughter? What drift had he been hiding behind?

I wiggled against the glob of snow that was trying to pull me in deeper, praying I didn't look as ridiculous as I pictured in my mind. What kind of an inept woman got stuck in a snowdrift?

Sydney didn't notice my hostage situation, so she took off down the unshoveled sidewalk. *Thanks for that.* I rolled to my stomach and pushed my way free from the ground, and in the process, my hat slid over my forehead and into my eyes.

"Need a hand?"

How did that charming voice get right in front of me that quickly?

Suddenly my hat was pulled from my head, certainly sending my limp, plain-old-brown hair flying in every direction. Standing in front of me was a broad chest covered by a red Columbia coat. My vision traveled up to find Mr. Be Still My Heart grinning at me.

Words. Where were those dumb words when I needed them?

"Hi." Yep. That was all I managed. One stupid *hi.*

He chuckled. "Hi there. You okay?"

"Yep."

He stood, his hand still hovering above my head with my hat between his fingers. "Would you like your hat back?"

"Yes."

"Okay." His other hand came up, and he snugged the stocking cap back over my ridiculous hair. "Better?"

I nodded. "Thanks."

Movement of pink and camo-green hues at my side

distracted me from my completely zoned-in stare at his beautiful blue eyes.

Syd tugged my hand, and I looked at her. "Mom, you're being weird."

Oh good. Ridiculous and weird. And called out by my seven-year-old. This was going super well.

"Yeah, I think you smashed my head, kiddo." I rubbed at her hat, begging God that this man who'd made me all mushed up bought my outright lie. I thought that God probably said no, seeing as lying was a sin.

"You're brutal, Syd-monster." He patted her shoulder. "Don't even know your own strength."

"I know, right?" Syd did her version of a hop.

It looked awkward. Had it always looked awkward? I really did need to have a talk with Joe.

Mr. Gorgeous robbed that thought of any hope for action. "So, is this your house?"

"Yes." Sydney grinned and then pointed next door. "Is that yours?"

"No, two doors down, and it's my aunt's. I stay with her when I'm working in Rock Creek."

"Mrs. Rustin is your aunt?" I grinned, partly because, *yay*, I could speak like an adult to this man, and then there was the fact that Mrs. Rustin was one of my favorite people. Kind, outspoken, and loved by just about everyone in Rock Creek. Having the same blood in his veins was definitely a bonus for Craig Erikson. Not that he needed it.

"Yes, ma'am. How lucky am I?"

"Pretty darn." I was on a roll now. All adultish and witty.

His charming mouth still fixed with a grin, he glanced away, his eyes finding Sydney, and then seemed to think for a moment. "So you know my cousin, Paul, right?"

"Yes. I know Paul and his wife, Suzanna. She's the reason we have the Java Palace now. She set Ruthie up with the distributor, and all the coffee addicts in Rock Creek rejoiced."

Chuckling, Mr. Erikson nodded. "I'll bet. The two of them can down a gallon in a single morning, easily. I can't keep up."

I squinted a mocking look of disapproval. "You don't drink coffee?"

"Not much."

"That's not normal, I think. I don't know if we can be friends."

He molded the most adorable puppy pout. "That's tragic. How can I change your mind?"

My heart grabbed on to his charm and did a twirl. Mr. Hotter-than-Most wanted to be my friend. Possibilities plinked through my head. What if...

That box—still unopened and in my bag—floated through my imagination.

No. He'd called me *Mrs.* yesterday. Had known nothing about me. I glanced at Sydney. She was not much of a secret keeper. Wasn't likely that her newest favorite toy didn't know anything about her life, and by extension, mine.

Which left the possibilities wide open.

"I've got a proposal for you."

My heart heard *something something something*

proposal and then stopped. Suddenly my knees wobbled again.

"What do you think?"

Oh. He'd kept talking, even though I'd stopped listening. "Uh, say that again."

"Paul's got a great sledding hill. We used it as kids, when it was his grandparents' place. How about you and Syd head out that way with me tomorrow? I can call Dre, and we can make a day of it."

A day at the Rustin ranch with all the Rustin kids. Syd would call it a ten.

Add Craig Erikson, and I'd call it off the charts. "That might make up for the coffee problem."

His smile spread full again, and his attention drifted to Sydney. "What do you say, kiddo?"

"'Bout what?"

I looked over to the daughter I'd lost track of. She sat with her legs sprawled out, an armory of snowballs on either side of her hips.

"Tomorrow you and your mom head out to my cousin's ranch with me to go sledding?"

A sly smile crept across her mouth. "I say you just saved yourself from a bombing. For now."

"What?" He stepped her way. "You wouldn't dare."

"You don't know me so good."

"That's it." One last step and he had my squealing girl swept up in his arms and turned upside down.

"Your mom gets to pick the drift, and you're going in head first."

Sydney wiggled like a fish on a hook. I laughed, except inwardly I fought away panic. He didn't know the extent of her leg issues, didn't know he needed to be careful.

"What do you say, Mom?"

I caught his eye and drew in a breath, subtly shaking my head. His eyebrows tugged in quizzically, and then he turned her right side up.

"Hey." Still in his arms, Syd leaned toward his face. "What happened?"

Mr. Erikson leaned in too. "Were you really going to throw snowballs at me?"

"Maybe."

"Hmm." He glanced at me and then scrunched his nose, refocusing on her. "Here's the deal. You and me against Paul and Keys. You'd better bring your best game."

Sydney puckered a Shirley Temple scowl. "You're on, Mr."

"Good." He bent to set her down, making sure she was steady on her feet before he let go, and then turned to me. "Are you any good at launching a snowball?"

I shrugged. "I can toss a few."

"Perfect, 'cause Suzanna's got a gun in her right arm."

I laughed, shaking my head. "I'll bet Suz and I will be inside drinking coffee while you're at war."

"Huh." He walked back to my side. "We'll see about that."

I ran out of words. Dang it.

After an extended pause, Mr. Erikson nudged my arm. "Take you out around nine?"

Take me out? Like a date? Such a featherbrain. He was talking about tomorrow. We'd ride with him to the ranch.

Was that like a date?

"Well?"

I glanced up at him. Those eyes...I melted again. "That'll work." I employed my best mom-to-teacher voice. "Thank you, Mr. Erikson."

"Craig." He turned to face me straight on. "You only get to come if you call me Craig."

"Got it." I smiled. "Craig."

With a gloved index finger, he tapped my nose. "Prefect, Kale. I'd better go finish the drive, but I'll see you tomorrow."

I think I muttered a *bye*, but I wasn't sure. My mind was too busy juggling thoughts about shoveled driveways and how *Craig* and *Kale* fit together.

Poetically. In a Dr. Seuss sort of way.

Chapter Four

I'd nearly wished I hadn't texted my parents and made a lunch commitment. I could have invited Craig in for hot chocolate and made something up for lunch.

No, never mind that. I wasn't sure he was the grilled cheese sandwich type. And hot chocolate was Joe's thing.

"Are we really going out to the Rustins' tomorrow?" Sydney shook snow off her hat onto the hardwood floor.

"Syd, don't. Now we're going to need to mop up the wet spots."

She looked down at her feet and shrugged. "Are we?"

"Sounds like it." I snatched a dish towel from near the kitchen sink and dropped to my hands and knees in front of her. "Hold still now, and don't drop any more snow everywhere."

"We hardly ever go out there. Just for the fall hayride. Will the big girls be there, do you think?"

Words were not adequate to express how much Sydney adored Kelsey and Kiera Kent. She tolerated their little brother, Keegan, but Kels and Keys were royalty as far as Syd was concerned.

"That's what Craig said."

Sydney wrinkled her nose. "Craig?"

"Mr. Erikson."

"You call him Craig?" One sassy little eyebrow tipped

toward her hairline.

Uh...what to say to that? I focused on the snow cleanup under my hands. "Sure. I call Jane by her first name. And Joe. Why not Craig?"

"He's my teacher, Mom."

Such a mouth. My seven-year-old sounded like a fifteen-year-old. I glanced up at her and rolled my eyes. "Yes, daughter. And Joe is your physical therapist. Same thing."

"Humph."

I puzzled over her reaction as I climbed off my knees and walked the dirty towel to the laundry. Not what I would have expected from the girl who gushed over this man. Then again, maybe it would be weird to have your mom be friends with your favorite teacher. She hadn't objected to the trip out to the Rustin ranch though.

Little girls. Who could figure them?

"Are we going to Gram's soon? I'm getting hot."

"Yes, Princess Hurry Up." I pinched her nose and then moved back to the kitchen to finish loading my canvas grocery bag. "I would have been ready five minutes ago if you hadn't shaken snow all over."

Sydney lifted her best angelic smile to me and tugged her hat back onto her hair. "Bet I'll beat you there."

She was always in a hurry, that girl. So sad that she really couldn't go that fast at all. Joe had a point, and I still hadn't called him. Maybe tonight. Definitely. He'd be done with work, so I wouldn't be pestering him then.

I slung the straps of my bag over my shoulder and

replaced the gloves I'd taken off. Stopping at the door to slip on my boots, Sydney and I set out to walk the five blocks to my parents' house. Snow still drifted downward from the sky, dancing with grace rather than with fury now that the wind had cut back. White blanketed everything like a clean sheet, and as we walked, I inhaled the cold crispness of winter.

I'd never been a fan of winter before. The cold, the need to bundle up, the naked landscape often covered in a monotony of snow. Not for me. And yet I remained in a winter-prone environment. Hadn't been my plan. None of my life, come to think of it, had been scripted. Go to school, fall in love, move somewhere warm, become the greatest mom ever...

Failure happened somewhere in the midst of step one and two. Probably should have been more particular about the falling-in-love part and more insistent on the finishing school. But none of that mattered. I had a seven-year-old daughter and adult bills to take care of, not to mention, my mom and dad needed me around. Snow was going to be a locked-in part of my life.

I visually grazed the landscape again, breathing once more the distinct cold freshness that came with a new coating of snow. It was pretty. Maybe even beautiful— this landscape of white and the still, cold air that came with it.

Beautiful might be a stretch.

My attention fell on the little girl ten feet ahead of me, now turning to hobble-run up the sidewalk toward her grandparents' front door. Not all game changers were bad.

She amazed me. I'd never once seen her mope about

her legs, whine about her braces. There'd been tears—sometimes brought on by the physical pain and sometimes by the emotional wounds delivered by a few punk kids—but on the whole, she'd been amazingly resilient. And determined. She faced life fearlessly, which terrified me. My fear issues seemed to have quadrupled to make up for her lack. I'd become helicopter mom and probably had bubble wrapped my kid.

Could you blame me? What mother wouldn't? From the moment I heard a stomach-turning crash followed by my two-year-old daughter's heart-stopping scream piercing the evening air, my life had shifted. Running from the bathroom to find her pinned under a bookshelf I'd been pestering Brad about anchoring to the wall, I knew two things for sure: I was the worst mom on the planet, and if she lived through that accident, I'd never let anything happen to Sydney again.

That got complicated, the last part. How could I never let anything happen to her without taking away her life?

Five years later, I still hadn't figured it out. In fact, it just kept getting more complicated.

I pushed the ever-circling problem aside. For today, the snow was beautiful-ish, Sydney was happy, and I was going to enjoy a visit with my parents.

***

I paused inside the door, one boot half off. Joe sat on the floor at my dad's feet, and for half a breath his eyes connected with mine. He didn't smile before he looked away, and he seemed unusually focused on the stretching routine he did with Dad.

Apparently the snow storm hadn't interfered with his twice-a-week house call.

"Let me take that bag, Kale." Mom lifted the straps from my arm. "It was so sweet of you to bring us lunch."

"Sure." I stripped my eyes from the back of Joe's head, irritated with the churn of guilt in my stomach. I *was* going to call him, bless it. I really was—just hadn't gotten there yet. But why'd he think he still had the right to be mad at me? I was, in fact, Sydney's mom and should have been asked.

Sydney finished kicking off her snow pants and marched straight over to the PT session happening in the den. Joe looked into her face and grinned. Nothing wrong between them.

A mild pain sparked in my chest.

"How's my favorite patient—no offense, Mr. Brennan." Joe winked at Syd and then looked up to my dad.

Dad chuckled. A good sign. He was following today.

"I'm awesome, as always."

Joe chuckled. "Ever humble too." He patted the floor beside him. "How about you do your stretches while your pops works on his?"

"I'd rather help you with his."

"Nope. I'll put ten bucks on the fact that you haven't done your exercises yet today." He leaned in, his nose nearly touching hers. "Have you?"

My spunky flower wilted. "No."

"What'd we talk about?"

Sydney flopped onto her back. "Working harder to get stronger, and maybe I won't need my braces next year."

Was he serious? He hadn't mentioned that to me. Drawing a long breath, I finished pulling off my own snow pants and walked toward the kitchen in the back of the house. Irritation and excitement played ping-pong in my brain as I passed the trio and their PT session.

Life without leg braces for Syd? That would be awesome. Was she really ready for it? Joe should have told me. Why wouldn't he? I had every right to know, and as my daughter's therapist, he had a responsibility to tell me.

Why was Joe being so weird?

Irritation was winning the round. I set to butter sliced Wonder Bread, making an attempt to follow the conversation my mom had started about a new quilt she and the girls were working on, but the battle in my head continued its back-and-forth storm.

Sydney was making progress—getting stronger. That was great.

Joe was being elusive and yet intrusive at the same time. We'd always gotten along well—even when we didn't agree, he'd at least been up front with me. *What gives?*

After checking the heat on the griddle iron with my palm hovering over it, I began slapping bread onto the surface. The butter sizzled, sending up that yummy aroma of grilled sandwiches that I'd never outgrown. I reached for the block of Colby Jack cheese, but a larger, masculine hand beat me to it. I looked up over my shoulder to find Joe stepping into the spot next to me. He unwrapped the cheese and set it on the slicer, silent as he ran the thin wire through the block.

Without looking at me, he passed the first slice my way. "Still mad at me?"

My lower jaw jutted to the side, and I bit my bottom lip, glancing at his face. He didn't look at me. "I haven't decided yet."

Another slice floated from his hand to mine, and I placed it on a waiting bread face. "Let me know when you're done."

Smug. Jerk. "You know what? Where do you get off, making decisions for my daughter without talking to me?"

"What?"

"Shoving her down a hill on a sled without my permission. Putting dreams in her head about things she's not ready for. Who do you think—"

"She's ready." Joe stopped slicing and turned a scowl down on me. "Or at least she could be, if we push her a little more."

Crossing my arms, I matched his scowl. "So I hold her back?"

His eyes flickered something intense mixed with a tinge of anger. "Sometimes."

I glared at him but locked my mouth shut. After a breath, I turned back to the sandwiches, which were ready to be turned, and wielded my lifter none too gently.

It wasn't like I didn't know he was right. But why—

"Kale." Joe's fingers brushed down my arm. "Look. I didn't mean—"

"I already know, Joe. Okay? I'm not what she needs. I lay awake at night with that thought spinning a web of failure in my head. I know I'm not the greatest mom."

His hand gripped my elbow and tugged, forcing me to face him. "That is not true."

Blinking—because, dang it, now tears were threatening—I looked into his eyes. "I hold her back, make her the bubble kid. That's what you said. My fear keeps her from getting better, stronger."

Suddenly his shoulders sagged, and he exhaled a long breath. Remorse replaced the irritation in his expression, and he shook his head before wrapping an arm over my shoulders. "You're amazing, Kale. I didn't mean for you to take it like that. I'm sorry." He squeezed my shoulders, and then in an unorthodox move, he pulled me into a full hug.

Maybe not unorthodox. He'd hugged me before. Before surgeries, and after them. Even had prayed with me, his hands locked over mine. But those weren't the same. I couldn't identify why, but they didn't feel the same.

I tucked my forehead against his chest. His soft sweater felt warm, and the hint of his calming cologne invited me to stay. My stomach did a little twirly thing when his hold tightened. That unidentifiable feeling suddenly birthed an unbidden thought: *If I tipped my face up, would he—*

Stop right there. That was so wrong, for lots of reasons. First off—I was totally crushing on Craig Erikson, not Joe White. Only junior high girls did that with two men at once. And second—I needed Joe as my friend, for

Sydney's sake. The one who would challenge my fears, call me out on my stubbornness. What he did for Sydney was so much more than physical therapy, and he was about the only person, doctors included, who would stand up to me for her sake. We needed him, so I had better not mess things up.

Which explained why I was still snuggled up to him in a way-friendlier hug than *just friends* enjoyed.

Step away from the gentleman, and no one will get hurt.

Still I stalled, until the smell of burning bread snapped me into obedience. I took a healthy step back, refusing to look at him, and recaptured the lifter I'd set down beside the stove. Joe let me go, crossed his arms, and leaned his backside against the counter.

"So...Syd says you're going out to the Rustins' place tomorrow." His easygoing tone returned.

I nodded, stumbling my way back to casual with less ease. "Yeah. Craig Erikson invited us. I guess Paul's his cousin."

"He mentioned that." Joe leaned on his palms, braced against the counter. "Are you going to let Syd go sledding?"

I drew a cleansing breath and glanced up to his open expression. "You really think she's ready?"

"You know I wouldn't have put her on that disk if I didn't."

I did know that. Which made me a crazy, overprotective mother bear. "Yeah. I know." I sighed. "I don't think I want her on that thing they pull behind the four-wheeler though."

"Good call." He nodded with a small grin. "She'll be

fine on a short hill. Just remind her to be sure everyone below is clear, and she's safer on her own. No double rides."

I wished Joe was going too.

No I didn't. That might be awkward.

Yes I did. There was nothing awkward about it. He was my friend.

The ping-pong game ensued while I loaded a platter with sandwiches. Once it was full and the griddle was empty, Joe took the meal to the table, and the afternoon moved forward. He stayed—which surprised me a little—playing Skip-Bo with Sydney and my dad until late afternoon. Apparently he only worked with his older patients on a snow day because losing a day was a much bigger deal for them than the younger ones. He'd already taken care of what he needed to earlier that morning.

I busied myself with my mom as we prepared several meals for their freezer. I wanted to have them stocked, just in case I couldn't stop by. Especially since I hoped to catch some extra hours at the Java Palace the next week, which would mean Syd would be hanging out with them. That needed to be the least amount of work possible for my mom, and ready-made meals were a good start.

With practiced efficiency, I formed several meatloaves, letting my mind wander. It circled around a man who made my knees weak with one amazingly beautiful smile. But hearing a different man laugh at the table in the next room stole the schoolgirl sigh from my lungs.

I wondered why I felt disappointed.

Chapter Five

Blue skies greeted us the next morning. Wished the murky clouds in my head had cleared along with the winter storm. I brushed them aside as I pulled the bake-from-a-can cinnamon rolls I'd splurged on out of the oven.

The clouds remained heavy in my mind. Joe...what was going on there? Craig was taking us out today. Sort of on a date-ish kind of thing. And I liked him—his presence thrilled me. Not to mention that gift, which still hid in my purse, unopened. It was driving me crazy, but I wasn't sure I wanted to know what was in it or who had left it.

Craig did. Probably. And that should thrill my stupid heart until it puddled. Should. Didn't mean it did. And that made me...dizzy? Frustrated? Disappointed? All of the above.

With a yawn and then a smile, Sydney limped down the hall without her braces strapped from her feet to her upper calves. Only ever in the morning did she move around without them, and not for very long at that. Her legs were still weak, and when she was actively growing, the pull on the bone grafts ached something terrible. Without those leg braces, she simply hadn't been strong enough to last a whole day on her feet.

But Joe said...

Joe didn't hold her while she whimpered after a day when she'd done too much.

I squeezed my eyes shut, banishing all thoughts—good and bad—of Joe White.

"Does your head hurt, Mom?"

Fixing my attention on her little body squirming into a chair, I smiled and shook my head. "Just thinking too hard."

"Well, don't do that. It's Saturday, and we're going places."

My chest moved with a quiet chuckle. The little sass. Such a gift God gave her—that spitfire personality. She had definitely needed it in her young, hospital-filled, challenge-laden life.

"Right. Start with breakfast. And hot chocolate."

No arguments there. She wolfed down two rolls and the sliced orange I'd set on her plate, and had her cocoa nearly finished within ten minutes.

"Snow day, part two!" She popped out of her chair. "I get to sled, right?"

"If you remember what Joe told you."

"Course I do. I always listen to him."

Right. "So you've done your stretches this morning?"

Her shoulders drooped, and she let her head fall back. "Blah. Not you too."

"Yes, me too. Get after it." Look at me being the tough, *let's get it done* kind of mom. *Ha, take that, Mr. You're Too Soft on Your Daughter.*

I instantly felt guilty for such a snarky thought. Had he heard me, Joe would have been hurt. He only wanted what was best for Syd. And he was usually right.

Saving me from guilt, Sydney hollered from her bedroom. "What time is Mr. Erikson going to come?"

"Soon." I peeked at my reflection in the microwave oven. It'd been silly to fix my hair. We'd be out in the cold with hats on most of the day, but I fingered the soft, loose curl I'd wrapped in my boring, straight hair earlier that morning. Maybe it'd stay bouncy, hanging out from under my crocheted cap, like those beautiful women you saw in those cutesy greeting card commercials.

A girl could dream. In reality, my lifeless locks would hang flat and stringy against my purple winter coat within thirty minutes of our sledding adventure. Some women were just not endowed with adorableness.

I sighed, moving away from my reflection, and headed to the dryer. Our winter gear waited in the tumbler, where I'd left them last night. Hopefully dry, Syd and I would start layering them on as soon as she was done working those tender little muscles. With my arms loaded with winter garb, I stopped to peek in on her progress. She sat in her undies with her legs flat on the floor, toes tipped toward her little body in what I knew as the staff pose. Her lips moved as she whispered numbers to herself, and I watched my little girl being responsible.

My eyes traveled over the scars littering her lower tibia and then the longer incision scar poking out of her underwear on her hip. I blinked against the tears. My baby had endured so much pain in her young life, and it was my fault. I should have been watching her. I should have been right there...

But I hadn't been, and Sydney's lower tibias had been shattered as a result. Since that awful day, she had endured five surgeries, two of them bone grafts that involved both the bone and marrow in her hip. Relearning how to walk had the added difficulty of excruciating pain in both her hips and her lower legs.

My chest locked down, and breathing became hard. If only...

"Whatchya doing?"

Startled, I looked at Sydney's face. Her eyebrows tilted in her *you're being weird* look, and I pushed away from the doorway in an attempt to recover myself. "Just making sure you're doing them right."

"I am." She lay on her back and placed her feet flat on the floor next to her bottom. "Watch this one." Up she went, all the way to her tiptoes. She held for five, her little legs trembling, and then dropped down to her heels. "I'm s'posed to work up to twenty. Maybe by Christmas."

Christmas. Seemed like so many hopes wrapped up in that one day. As it should be, maybe, but usually...

This Christmas would be special. Different. It'd be amazing for Syd. Somehow, I'd make it amazing.

"Okay, one set done." Sydney, who had apparently done more reps while I'd mentally wandered off, was on her feet again. "Can that be all for now?"

I was about to nod, and then changed my mind. "What would Joe say?"

Sydney grinned. "Joe's not here."

"Joe wants some pretty great things for you. Maybe we should listen."

With her chin tilted in a bit of a sassy look, Sydney raised her eyebrows. "Since when..." Her voice trailed off, and then a small grin crept over her lips. "Maybe we *should* pay more attention to him."

What was my monkey-head conjuring up now? "Do another set, and then get dressed. Craig will be here soon."

"You mean Mr. Erikson."

"Yes. Mr. Erikson to you. Get going."

By the time Craig arrived, Sydney was nearly dressed. I invited him in and offered him a cup of coffee.

Craig waved it off. "That would be Paul and Suzanna's thing, not mine."

I nodded, replacing the mug I'd already pulled from the cupboard. Mr. Erikson stood on the entry rug, dressed in his snow garb and dwarfing my house with his overwhelming presence. As I'd only met him outside, I didn't fully comprehend the man's large stature until this moment. *Tim Tebow meets Mr. Rogers indeed.* The guy was huge.

"So..." He glanced around my small bungalow house, what he could see of it. "This is home?"

I felt like a tiny person living in a tiny house with my tiny life. "Such as it is."

Silence slithered around us, twisting with uncomfortable bends.

I took a stab at conversation, because something needed to kill the awkwardness. "Where is home for you?"

"All over, really." He chuckled, one hand snatching his snow hat off his head. "My stuff is actually still at my mom's place. I haven't gotten around to finding one all my own. But I'm hardly ever there. I travel the region and land back at what I guess you'd consider home maybe twice a month."

No home? Bizarre. And maybe a little sad. "What keeps you away?"

"My job, which is my choice, so don't feel bad or anything. I like what I do."

"What is that exactly?"

His smile broadened, and I remembered that gooey feeling from the other day, because my knees reminded me.

"My degree is in elementary music education, and I have a minor in special ed. But what I do now is probably closer to entertainment than what I studied for. I've managed to gain open invitations to a large number of school districts in the western part of the state, and I travel around as sort of a special-specials teacher."

How did a guy with that build wind up as a music teacher? I didn't have time to ask him, because Sydney wandered from her room, all winterized from head to toe.

"All right, Mr. Erikson." She grabbed his hand and swung him around with her tiny little self so that he faced the door. "Snowflake party, part two. Hit it."

"Yes, ma'am."

She yanked the door open and tugged him behind her. "Coming, Mom?"

Yep. Off we went. Snowflake party, part two. Sydney was clearly thrilled to her damaged little feet about this arrangement. So why exactly did she insist I call this massive hero of hers *Mr. Erikson*?

Her quirks didn't make any sense.

***

Craig was right. Suzanna could throw a snowball like a bullet from a rifle. She outplayed me shamelessly, and her laughter gave me a little insight as to why Paul had pursued her even when everyone else in town thought she was about as nice as a rattler in October.

Guess everyone had scars. We just wore them in different places and with different bandages to hide them. Suzanna had worn hers with anger overtop.

Me? I didn't know how mine looked to others. Didn't pause life long enough to consider it, but after Suzanna had given me an olive branch of grace by offering me an out of this snowball war I wasn't good at and didn't love, I suddenly wondered. About her and about me.

"Where'd you learn to throw like that?" I asked as she set a pot of coffee to brew. "Did you play softball or something?"

A sad, reserved smile smoothed her lips as she turned to me. "My first husband. He played baseball in college."

Hold everything. Suzanna had been married? Before Paul? Didn't seem possible. She wasn't that much older than me, and she'd been Suzanna Wilton—same last name as her dad—before she became Suzanna Rustin.

"I know. I should have told people." Suzanna slid into the chair across from mine, and a small pause filled the space.

Andrea had stayed outside, determined to pummel her brother with the white stuff. Boy, if ever there were opposites, Suzanna and Andrea were it. Dre was known as the fun, *live it up but be nice* kind of woman. She was the kind of person everyone wanted at a party.

Suzanna...was growing on me.

"What happened?"

"He died. Cancer. I was pretty devastated. My family had fallen apart. My mom and I have had a rough past, and Jason—my first husband—was my safe place." She sat back, her gaze steady. Clearly she'd worked through some things since she'd first settled in Rock Creek two years before. "I really thought that God hated me. All these disappointments in my life—I felt like I was completely alone. That He didn't notice me, and if He did, He just flat out wasn't interested."

Her confession triggered an avalanche of memories. Bad ones. Multiple nights of ongoing fights. Tears. Pleading. As if dealing with the extent of Sydney's injuries hadn't been enough.

"That's what Brad thought..." I whispered.

Suzanna held my gaze, her silence inviting me to continue. "Brad is Syd's father. We were together until a few months after Sydney's accident. He was never really the faithful church type, but I thought he'd grow into it, and since I prayed that Jesus would save him, I figured it was just a matter of time... I guess it was. Sydney's accident turned him ice cold. At first he started praying—no demanding—'God, heal her. We can't do this.' Then..."

I paused, tears fogging my vision. "Syd didn't get better. In fact, when her first cast came off and they re-x-rayed her leg, the news got worse. A lot of the bone fragments were dead. She needed transplants, and it was going to be a long process.

"He quit. Said God was either not real or didn't care, and he wasn't built for this kind of hard life. He quit us both."

A mutual hush bonded us as we waited for the drip brew to gurgle. When I looked up, Suzanna's kind blue eyes were already settled on me.

"You've walked a tough path, Kale. I'm so sorry."

I tried to brush off her compassion, because it made me self-conscious. "Well, you did too."

"Looks like you've fared a bit better than I did." She traced the grain of her kitchen table. "I was one bitter, lonely woman."

"I had Syd and my parents, so..." I hesitated, wondering how much prying would be out of line. Suzanna had opened up first though. "Did Paul change things for you?"

She laughed, moving to pour the coffee into two mugs. "That's a complicated question, with a not-so-clear answer. Paul, and his family, embodied everything that I longed for—stability and acceptance. Love. But it wasn't enough. Even when I knew Paul loved me, it just didn't fill the hole." She chuckled, shaking her head. "He said I was like a leaky water trough and he couldn't fix me."

The mug made a hollow thud against the table as she set it in front of me.

"So what happened?"

"I left. Spent some more time yelling at God, not

believing that He was listening, that He cared about me. And then—"

"What?" I leaned forward.

"I saw Him. The real God, the One who had been waiting for me to fall into His arms the whole time."

I traced the handle of my mug. What had that been like, to see God—to fall into His arms? I'd never stopped believing in Him, but...well, I often thought He didn't see me. I was too insignificant. My life didn't matter that much.

"How?" I asked before realizing the word came out of my mouth. Clearing my throat, I glanced to my coffee. "I mean, how do you fall into His arms?"

Suzanna folded her hands and rested her elbows on the table. "I'm not sure I know how to explain it. But I guess I kept expecting Him to show up in the big moments. To save Jason. Fix my family. When He didn't, resentment set in. But, well, maybe we shouldn't *just* be looking for God in those big moments, because if we can't see Him in the small everyday things, we won't be able to understand that He's there right beside us in the moments that cave in our lives."

My throat swelled as I processed her story—her assessment. Life had caved in on me, and honestly, I didn't think I'd recovered. I wasn't angry, but I hadn't looked for God's hand in it either. I guess I hadn't expected it to be there.

A burst of cold air and a chorus of laughter broke the moment between Suzanna and me, but I felt our bond tie secure. As the group stumbled into their house, noisy and with their cheeks and noses red from the cold, I set aside the deep wonderings our conversation had stirred.

Sydney stumbled through the entry door between Kelsey and Kiera, her face lit like a Christmas tree and her smile as bright as a star. Looked like we'd both had a good day. Craig lumbered in behind them, his grin aimed at me.

Drawing a long breath, I wondered about his life, why he'd chosen the path he was on and if he was running from something. Didn't seem likely, given his joyous personality, but you never knew what lay behind a smile.

Chapter Six

Sydney gave us a small opportunity to talk on the drive back to town. She crashed, completely wiped out, in the back of the car before we made it around the first turn.

"Thanks for the fun today, Craig."

"I had a blast, so don't thank me."

There seemed to be no end to his energy. His enthusiasm animated his voice.

"Syd hasn't had such a fun day in ages." Inwardly I groaned, wondering how much pain she'd be in that night. Exhaustion settled in, and I tipped my head back, my attention sliding to the treeless white expanse beyond my window.

Being absorbed into the Rustin clan had been a bit surreal. The rest of the afternoon had been filled with stories, amazing tomato soup, the likes of which I'd never tasted, and more fun for Syd than she'd have in a month with her overprotective, boring mom.

Being there with Craig, however, made the day seem uncomfortable. Dre and Paul both seemed to assume that I'd somehow magically become their cousin's girlfriend overnight. Craig seemed to be fine with it. I was stuck playing another round of mental ping-pong.

What gives on that anyway? Here I had this incredibly good-looking man take me out to meet his extended family for a day packed with fun, and I was dissecting every conversation between him and me, looking for flaws and expecting a bad ending.

Must have been hold-over emotions from Brad. Hard to believe men could be truly good when a guy left a hole that big in your life.

I didn't miss Brad—not like I did when he first left. But I missed the idea of him and me together forever. I missed the fairy tale that had shattered right along with Sydney's legs. Ideal family, mommy and daddy standing strong in the storm. I didn't get that one—and I knew it wasn't all Brad's fault. But it was hard not to measure every man by his failures.

And to be honest, Craig seemed too good to be true. Men like that—they had big dreams. Extraordinary lives.

My life didn't have a place in that kind of picture. Too ordinary to be special. Too complicated to be extraordinary.

These thoughts swirled through my head as we continued on the gravel roads back toward town.

"You're a quiet one, aren't you?"

I pulled my attention away from the white expanse and looked at Craig. He glanced at me, his look inviting, before he returned his attention to the road.

"Sorry."

"It was an observation, not a put-down." He smiled. "Just surprised me a bit. Syd isn't."

I looked back at my daughter, still bundled in her winter gear. With her head tipped back and her mouth slightly open, she looked like a bundle of peace.

"No, she's not quiet. Syd is full of spunk, and she's got more words than most."

"She's fun. I was looking forward to seeing her again when I was coming this way."

I settled back in my chair. "Yeah, we were talking about that—about you traveling and your work. Didn't get to finish."

"Not much more to tell. Somehow I landed in this gig, and it's a pretty good fit. I get to be everyone's favorite guy, so..."

"I'm sure that was true before." *Look at me being bold.*

He rewarded my forwardness with a wink. "Depends on who you talk to."

Hmm. What did I do with that bait?

He didn't give me time to decide. "So the parade tonight..."

I waited, my eyebrow raising. "Was there a question in there?"

"Just wondered if you and Syd would hang out with me. I've never been to Rock Creek's parade of lights."

Laughter escaped from my nose, which surely was not attractive. "Well, don't be late, or you'll miss it. But the party at the old barn in town is pretty fun."

"Was that a yes or a no?"

I blinked, examining the profile of his good-looking face. Strong jaw, stubbled with whiskers from his evening shadow. Rather sharp nose, but it fit well on his face. And that puddle-me-gooey smile.

Why would he be interested in me?

He glanced at me again, blue eyes mesmerizing me in an instant. "Do I get an answer?"

"Yes."

His head tilted toward me. "Yes, you'll answer me, or yes, that's your answer?"

"Yes." I giggled again, finally comfortable with this man after an entire day of unease.

With another look aimed my way, he molded a smirk on his face. "I'm going to take that as a yes, you're going with me."

"Okay."

He shot a look over his shoulder. "Will Sydney approve?"

"Will the sun come up tomorrow?"

"She won't think it's weird?"

She already thought it was weird. Didn't stop her from having the day of her life. "Nah. Syd rolls with life. It's God's best gift to her."

***

We met Craig on Main Street. That felt safer to me. When I told Sydney that we were going, she whooped. Then I mentioned Craig would be there—no, I said Mr. Erikson would be there. Her little eyebrows lifted toward her hairline, and then she said, "Okeydokey. If that's what you want."

What the heck did that mean?

She bounced—well, hobble-hopped—away from me, heading down the hall to her room. Next thing I knew, she was dressed in the snow clothes I'd once again tossed into the dryer after Craig dropped us off at home, and announced that she was "ready!" in her singsongy voice.

Leg braces or not, if only I could keep up with her.

The parade was typical. About twenty floats, strung up with Christmas lights, supported by local businesses, ranches, churches, and other organizations, slowly rolled down the street to "Frosty the Snowman" and "The Twelve Days of Christmas." As predictable as it was, one couldn't help but smile. Some small-town holiday traditions were priceless, even if it was literally freezing out.

"How about some hot chocolate?" Through chattering teeth, I looked first at Sydney and then at Craig, who had stood by my side but had made no other advancement other than small talk during the whole ten-minute parade.

He nodded. "Sounds good."

"We'll miss the piñata." Sydney scowled.

"A piñata?" Craig managed a look of both curiosity and amusement. "For Christmas?"

I giggled, a little self-conscious about my quirky small town. "Yeah. In the barn. It's a Rock Creek tradition. I think it's a Rudolph one this year."

"They put chocolate Santas in that thing." Syd tugged on his arm. "I can't miss that. Let's go."

Craig laughed. "Definitely can't miss that." He looked at me. His free hand dug into his pocket and then produced a twenty-dollar bill. "I'll take Syd, if you want to grab the cocoa?"

"Sure." I wanted to wave away the twenty. But, boy, things were tight...

I didn't know if he could sense my mental back and forth or not, but he leaned toward me and tucked the money into my coat pocket. "I insist." He winked and tapped my nose with a gloved finger.

My stomach spiraled. I wasn't sure it was all pleasure. Dating had been off my to-do list for a while. Brad had cut off a big part of my heart, and the rest had been dedicated to Sydney. I wasn't sure I was ready for this—or if I had the courage to learn to trust another guy.

Didn't mean I didn't pray for it though. Especially on those long nights when the guilt was especially loud, opening the deep hollow of loneliness along with all the other marks of failure littering my life. *God*, I would think, *is it possible to find favor in a good man's eyes when I'm a total mess?* The tears would begin to trickle somewhere in that silent prayer, a mixed bundle of emotions. I knew, *knew* with my head and my heart, the great compassion of my loving Father. He'd walked me through the darkest time of my life, with my daughter in the hospital and her dad AWOL. With complete certainty, I felt His arms around me in the deepest spots of loneliness.

But there were some days when I ached for the tangible touch of a man by my side. One who would take on my ordinary, super-challenging life with strength and valor. Who would see me, love me. Love my daughter. Did that make me weak? Ungrateful?

I didn't know. But at the moment, shivering in the cold with the possibility of maybe finding favor in Craig's eyes, I felt mostly terrified.

Still shivering from cold and emotions, I reached the Java Palace and took my place in the snake of a line trailing out the front door.

"You're not working." Joe nudged my shoulder from behind and then took the narrow empty spot on the sidewalk beside me.

I looked up and smiled, noting the easygoing friendliness in his dark-brown eyes. Not a trace of the tension that had been between us yesterday. With a half grin of relief, because I hated how much being at odds with him had messed with me, I shook my head.

"No. This must have been a last-minute decision for Ms. Ruthie." I rubbed the twenty in between my fingers. "Wish she'd called me though. I could use the hours."

"But then you'd miss the piñata..." His voice trailed off, and he glanced around. "Where's Syd?"

Tension returned. Tenfold. "She's up at the barn already. I think. She went with Cr—Mr. Erikson."

Joe studied me. For like almost a full minute. Felt that long, at least. And totally uncomfortable. Except maybe I didn't want him to look away because it was slightly possible that I kind of enjoyed his full attention set on me.

The line moved forward, and he nudged me through the entry, holding the door open. "How'd the day at the ranch go?" Nothing changed in his easygoing voice. Not a flicker in his kind eyes. Not a single hint of...

What?

Had I hoped it would matter to him that I'd—we'd spent the day with Craig?

Totally ridiculous. Joe had been at our sides for five years. Sixty months. Two hundred sixty weeks. Never once had I entertained such thoughts. And I didn't standing next to him, with his arm hovering over my shoulder while he held that door propped open. I inhaled the chilled scent of that calming aroma that rose from his nearby chest. Promise. Not one single thought of how maybe I hoped he might be a little jealous. Possessive of our rela—friendship. Nothing of the sort, because that would be juvenile. And unfair.

"We had fun. Craig"—yes, I used his given name like an adult and not to spark some kind of emotion out of Joe—"pulled Syd around the flats like he was in football training camp. And then we had a snowball fight. She loved it."

Joe nodded. The line moved again, and we followed, which allowed him to release the door, thus dropping his arm and removing my excuse to stand under it. Of course I wasn't disappointed.

"I'll bet she did." He pushed his hands into his pockets and looked down to his boots, hiding his expression under the tilt of his stocking-capped head. "What did you do?"

"Helped build a snowman. Rode the sled a couple of times. Got creamed in the snowball fight. Then went inside and drank coffee with Suzanna."

He chuckled quietly. "That sounds like you."

"What does?"

"Inside, drinking something warm. You're not much of a winter girl."

He'd noticed this about me?

"And coffee." He poked my arm with his elbow. "What would you be without coffee?"

I smirked. "You don't want to know."

He looked down the same moment I looked up, and our mutual glance stalled. Locked. He grinned with a mixture of knowing and laughter and depth that sank through the chill that had made me shiver the heartbeat before. Warmth oozed through me, and I couldn't remember what's his name with the charming smile and rather sharp nose, who was probably making my daughter giggle hysterically.

"Line's moving."

What line?

"Hey, if you're not going to order, can someone else go?"

I glanced backward, sadly disconnecting from those brown eyes that'd I'd seen at least twice a week for the last five years but had never studied before, for some dumb reason I couldn't explain. A high school boy with his arm snaked around a blond girl's neck stood back there, his eyebrows raised as if I'd gone stupid.

"What were you getting, Kale?" Joe had managed to move away from me while I looked at Mouthy Pants, and was waiting at the counter.

Awkward replaced that warm, comfy feeling. "Uh...hot chocolate."

Ruthie nodded. "One?"

"No." Long pause. "Three."

Ruthie glanced at Joe, a glimmer of a smile tugging on her mouth.

"I'll take one too," he said.

"In addition to her three?" Ruthie's smile dropped.

"Yes. No." He laughed. "One of my own. We're not together."

Three little words. True words. Words that should have been insignificant. My heart shrank.

"Right. Three for me. One for him." *Cute, Kale. Way to babble.* Apparently my intelligence shrank too.

Ruthie buzzed around behind the counter, and within two minutes we had our *separate* orders paid for and ready to go. I moved to tuck one of the capped cocoas into the crook of my elbow, but Joe took it from my hand.

"No reason to do that." He nodded his head to the side, indicating the exit. "I'm headed the same way."

I could have died. The last thing I wanted in the midst of my unexplainable confusion about both Joe and Craig was both Joe and Craig within spitting distance of me.

Muddled thoughts, that was all those were, because when we got to the barn, Craig was doing exactly what I would have guessed—cheering the kids on as they took big-league swings at the dangling Rudolph hanging battered from the center beam. He saw me come through the big double doors, with Joe trailing near my right side, and grinned. As we approached, Craig diverted his interest from the action in the middle to me and then Joe.

"Hey, buddy." Craig held out his right hand.

Joe met his offered civility with a mug of cocoa passed to him instead of a handshake. "Hey. Looks like we haven't missed all the fun."

"Nope. Just got started. Sydney is two spots back, so she'll get her turn in a minute."

I stood mute between the two men. On my right, Joe's stature reached a couple of inches above my head. Craig, on my left, towered over both of us with his six-four build. I felt sandwiched between Mr. Oh-So-Good-Looking-Not-to-Mention-Charming and Mr. Kind-and-Dependable-and-Why-Hadn't-I-Noticed-How-Warm-Those-Coffee-Eyes-Were? What was a girl to do?

Let me pause here to say that from the outside, this might have looked like an enviable position, and maybe in my flighty-young-woman stage of life I would have enjoyed toying with it. Let the record clearly state, however, that I was so tangled up inside that I felt sick.

There was no reason to feel nauseated though. Joe was, as ever, the nice man he'd always been. Friendly, respectful, and interested in others. He chatted with Craig about the college bowls coming up, about which team would most likely take the national championship, and about Craig's life as a college running back, which was all mildly fascinating and a good distraction from my knotted emotions.

Craig was chill. Included me in a natural way in the conversation, didn't act like a pit bull, and seemed to genuinely enjoy the setting and situation.

"Hold up." Joe spoke to Craig but tapped my arm midway through a sentence about UNL's current running back's bid for the NFL. "Syd's got the stick." He grinned, a mix of determination and pride passing over his face.

"She's got this, Kale." Craig also turned to face the center squarely, his attention set on my daughter. "Syd's one of the toughest kids I've ever met."

"See?" Joe's elbow poked my arm again. "What have I been telling you? She's got more in her."

I glanced up to him and his easy smile aimed at me before he looked back at Sydney. Apparently I was the only one of the three of us who felt a little odd in this scenario.

Of course I was—no one else had a reason to feel weird, and I didn't either. Joe was my friend. Craig was the one I'd come to the parade with. Sort of. This should not be confusing.

"Smack it, Sydney," Craig hollered.

Joe followed that up with, "Set those Santas free, Syd-monster."

At some point I figured I should probably join in the cheering. Although it seemed pretty well in hand by the two men flanking me.

Sydney's first whack landed on the tip of the poor deer's foot. The piñata shuddered, and she waited for it to stop bouncing. Swing two landed a solid blow in the middle, sending a telltale snapping sound through the room. The crowd yelled a collective "whoa!"

"Come on, kiddo." Joe chuckled. "You've got this."

"One more, Syd. It's all yours," Craig yelled.

It occurred to me as I glanced between the men, and then scanned the room full of people cheering for Sydney, that my daughter was exceptionally blessed. Losing, for a moment, my clutch on unease, a surreal gratitude filled my chest. Sydney was okay—more than okay. She'd battled an injury that had redefined her life from toddlerhood on, but she didn't really wear those scars on her heart. This girl of mine was funny and tough and friendly and lovable. She had everything she needed for a beautiful, productive life—with or without leg braces.

Tears glazed over my eyes, and in that moment, gratitude flooded my spirit, uprooting the ever-present power of guilt and regret.

Sydney was extraordinary. I was unbelievably proud. And humbled.

And grateful to the two men on either side of me, who didn't love on my kid because they felt sorry for her. They simply adored her, just because.

I wondered if this was what Suzanna had been talking about—looking for God in the everyday stuff. Something I definitely needed to practice more.

Chapter Seven

Every feat had its reward, and Sydney's was a triple portion of chocolate Santas stashed in my baking cabinet. To the victor belonged the spoils, though the other children in the barn the night before snatched up plenty. The town gave plenty—the benefits of living in a tight-knit community.

Other joys included lots of questions about things that would never go unnoticed.

"Did you go to the parade with Craig?" Andrea Kent asked before Sunday services started the following morning.

Dre was the last person on earth to start up a gossip line, but she was always the first one to ask if she had a suspicion about a situation. Blunt but genuine, and about as far from mean as the Arctic is from Hawaii, so though I was uncomfortable with her direct question, I wasn't irritated.

"We met there, yes. He bought Syd and I hot cocoa."

"Must have powered her up for the kill." Dre grinned. "That was a great swing."

"Thanks. She was pretty thrilled." I wrapped one arm

around my shoulder and tucked away my own proud grin.

Last night's realization about Sydney still swaddled my heart with tingles of joy. I'd actually slept fairly well the night before, the voices of guilt nearly drowned out by the burgeoning delight of wonder. My total negligence wasn't going to ruin her life. She took life and made what she wanted.

Maybe I could too.

Now to figure out what I wanted.

"Oh, I was just going to ask if you knew whether or not Craig was coming today, but there he is now."

Good. And bad. My heart started a reckless, uncoordinated tap dance. In my panic, my gaze darted around the church, landing on the one person in the room who would be able to calm my silent hysteria.

Not Jane.

Joe caught my glance, tossed a finger wave from his spot near a window to my right, and then returned to his conversation with Paul and Suzanna Rustin. The room stopped its swirling, and I was able to draw a long breath.

"Hi, Kale." Craig's gorgeous smile landed on me.

"Hey."

"Where's the champ? In a chocolate coma?"

I chuckled. "Surprisingly, no. Alice has her with the other kids. They're practicing for the Christmas Eve service."

Craig tilted his head. "She sings too? What can't she do?"

"Skip. Run. Hop." My soaring spirit plummeted. "You know, the hard stuff."

"Joe says she'll be doing those things before her next

birthday. Considering the trauma she's been through, I'd say she's doing amazing."

"Thanks." My smile felt false. How much did Joe discuss with Craig about Sydney? Did they talk about me?

"So, go with me to awkward for a moment, 'kay?"

I managed a raised brow and a nod before he plunged ahead.

"This is a small town, and I'm sure there's already talk. Doesn't bother me, but I don't live here, so for your sake, I'm going to sit with my aunt. But I wondered, before I go off and confuse you, if you'd be able to go to dinner with me tonight?"

A Sunday night date? In Rock Creek? Wasn't sure how he was going to pull that off. Be worth finding out.

"Sure. Let me check with my parents though." I swallowed, and heat burned my face. "Not that I need their...I mean." I cleared my throat, wanting to smack my forehead. "I need to see if Syd can hang out with them, is all."

He laughed and squeezed my shoulder. "Gotchya. Let me know if it doesn't work, and we'll figure something else out. I'd love a chance to get to know you better."

My pulse sputtered. A date. A real, actual date, with Mr. Charm himself.

I waited for my knees to wobble. It wasn't until I was sitting on the pew, and Joe slid onto the seat on my right, that I realized that swept-off-my-feet response wasn't going to happen.

***

"What are you looking for?" Joe leaned over and whispered in the space above Sydney's head.

I brought my attention back to the pulpit, where it should have been focused for the past twenty minutes. Something was off, and I couldn't set my mind where it ought to have been.

Sydney wiggled by my side, and I heard papers rustling. When I glanced down to see what she was up to, a folded note came my way, from Joe's hand stretched over Syd's lap.

With two fingers, I accepted it, giving him a sideways scowl. Passing notes in church? So not the dignified Joe White I knew.

What's wrong?

I glanced back to the door, scanned the last three rows with no change in sight, and then looked forward again, pausing when my sight landed on Craig near the front. Releasing a silent sigh, I took the pen from the pew in front of me and began scratching on the bulletin-turned-note.

My parents aren't here. Just worried.

The note floated between us again, and I watched out of the corner of my eye as Joe read it. His pen clicked, and he jotted a quick response.

Not that unusual. Maybe a bad day for your dad.

Yes. I knew. They were actually *my* parents. But today...

Another message, this time on his sermon notes, came my way.

What's up?

I didn't want to tell him. What if...

What if what? He felt bad that I was going out with Craig? Wasn't like he ever acted like there was anything between us.

With only the movement of my eyes, I looked at our knees gathered on the same bench. The three of us. Like we were...

Nothing.

It had been this way for the past couple of years. Joe always sat with Sydney and me. After the service, he'd ask her about the verse we learned from that day, sometimes challenge her to memorize it with him that week. That didn't mean he'd be upset about me going on a date. Besides, if he'd been interested, he'd had years to make it known. He hadn't, which meant he wasn't. So there was nothing to feel anxious about.

A nudge on my shoulder beckoned me out of my silent argument. With a glance to my right, I met Joe's inquisition. His eyebrows cocked in question, and his trademark kindness triggered a sense of safety where there had been angst. Leaning over the paper again, I put words to my problem.

Craig asked me to dinner tonight, but I don't want to ask Mom to keep Syd if Dad is having a rough time.

I reread what I'd written. How selfish can one woman be? With the slip still between my fingers, I sat back and debated...

And then the note was gone. Stolen by the guy sitting next to my daughter. Like he had the right to know.

Anxiety. Safety. Irritation. Joe was scoring well with my emotions.

Eyes forward, I couldn't look at him. With an exertion

of discipline I was usually unfamiliar with, I focused on the sermon.

"Don't get confused about where He is found. They looked for Him in a palace, but He was found in a manger. The mark of our good God is His extraordinary care for very ordinary people. When we look at the humility of the manger, the ordinary people He chose for the birth of Jesus, the lowliness of the first witnesses to that miracle, can it be denied? Our God is inexplicably enamored with us, even in our very ordinary lives."

Suddenly paying attention wasn't a challenge at all.

God's extraordinary care for ordinary people...

My vision slid from the pastor to the manger scene that had been sitting on the front stage since the week after Thanksgiving.

Away in a manger, no crib for a bed...

Didn't get much more ordinary than a humble birth to nobody parents. The extraordinary love of God tugged with precision on my heart. So many failures had marred my life up to that point. Some as a result of my willful disobedience. Some as a result of honest mistakes. Some as a result of life just being life. But in all of it, the God who loved ordinary people to the extent that He'd leave his glory to sleep in a manger of hay *loved me.* Before the failures that had altered the direction of my life, *He loved me.* And now in the common mess that defined my every day, *He loved me.*

Emotion crashed through my heart, and the guilt that had snarled around my spirit loosened its captive grip. I inhaled, shutting my eyes and savoring this feeling of joy.

"Run to the manger when you are sure He does not notice you. Know that He sees. And when you feel His gaze settled on you, turn to the cross. Know that He loves."

Pastor invited us to pray with him, and I was relieved for the privacy of every head bowed. My chest quivered within, and tears leaked through my closed eyelashes.

Teach me the joy of your extraordinary love. Teach me to see your hand in my everyday life.

I swiped the moisture under my eyes, removing all traces of my momentary collapse. By the time the corporate prayer ended, I had a decent grip on my swirling emotions. The benediction was given, and we were free to stand and chat. Only then did I remember the conversation via passed notes between myself and Joe.

He hadn't responded.

Facing forward, I couldn't help but see Craig turn toward me with his smile already in place. I'd have to tell him tonight wouldn't work, and while my chest sagged like a wet quilt on a clothesline, part of me felt a little relieved.

Perhaps I still wasn't ready.

"Kale."

I turned toward Joe, whose expression had gone reflective. He glanced toward the front of the room, his eyes following another person—probably Craig, who was walking our way, and then looked at me for one more quiet moment.

"I can stay with Sydney."

My heart stalled. And then it dropped and rolled. "Joe..."

"You wanted to go, right?"

I stared at him.

"It's not a problem. Syd and I can hang out." His hand settled on the head of dark hair belonging to the girl still standing between us. "We'll have fun."

Sydney looked up at him, but I couldn't see her face.

He returned her attention and gave a small grin. "Right?"

She drew a long breath, which meant her answer wasn't going to be a simple one. But then, after a pause much longer than I'd expected, she took his hand in hers and said, "Right. It'll be fun."

A full smile spread across his mouth, but he didn't make eye contact with me. I couldn't help but think that his expression seemed strained. Once again, his attention flitted away to a place just beyond my shoulder.

"It's settled then." Joe released Syd's hand and bumped my shoulder with his fist. "Just let me know what time." After a nod, not directed at me but at the person standing behind me, he turned and walked toward the door.

My head felt dizzy, and my thoughts jumbled together. Why would Joe do that? Why was I so preoccupied with him? And where had the Jell-O effect from Craig's smiles gone?

***

Sydney and I went straight to my parents' house after church. Between the swirl of thoughts about them and Craig and Joe, I felt off kilter. I needed to firm up at least one of the questions pounding in my brain.

Mom met me in the entryway, pale and a little sweaty. "Your dad took a fall this morning when he was walking to his chair."

Heart dropping, I looked over her shoulder across the room to where my dad rested, his feet kicked up in the recliner.

"Is he okay?"

She bit her lip. "I don't know for sure. He said to just let him sleep, so I did."

"Mom, why didn't you call me?" Slipping my coat off, and nodding Sydney toward the kitchen, I moved around her and headed toward my sleeping father.

"I knew you were in church, and you're always running to our rescue. He said to let him rest, that it wasn't an emergency."

I sighed, examining the old man who was just a shell of the guy I remembered. His mind had begun to slip a year after Sydney's accident. Little things, like not remembering how he took his coffee, became bigger, like forgetting my mom's name. To complicate his patchy mental condition, one day last year he'd taken himself out on a walk after a winter storm much like last week's. He'd slipped.

Probably easy to guess...broke his hip.

Recovering from that kind of injury at seventy years old could be tough. Or impossible.

"We should probably get over to urgent care, Mom." I rubbed my eyebrows, wishing she'd called me when it happened. "How on earth did you get him back up and into the recliner?"

"I'm no ninny." She crossed her arms. "And urgent care is over an hour away. He doesn't want to go."

"Mom. What if something's broken?"

"I don't think so." She stepped forward, running a hand over his thick silver hair.

"How can you know for sure?"

"I just don't think so, that's all. When he fell last year, he couldn't move the pain was so intense. Today, he just had a hard time getting back up. It's different."

"It's dangerous, Mom. We need to—"

"No. He said no, and he was thinking clearly. I'm going to honor those precious few moments."

"What about Joe, Mom?" Sydney appeared from the dining room, just beyond the den. "He could come check, right?"

Oh my word. My life seemed to be completely dependent on that man. I hadn't noticed or minded before, but with this Craig thing now...

Joe would come though, and he'd tell me honestly if I'd need to override my parents on this one.

One phone call made, and he arrived.

I wondered, as he assessed my dad with his calm, kind way, what he'd do if the Craig thing became a real, actual thing.

The thought made me a little sick. I couldn't imagine that kind of shift. Didn't really want to either.

***

"So...Joe."

Snuggling into a heavy quilt, I leaned back against an Adirondack chair in Andrea Kent's backyard. Clever man, that Craig Erikson. Tom and Dre were spending the evening in town with some friends, and Craig had snagged permission to use their farmhouse for our date. The bonfire in front of us crackled, its orange light an intense contrast to the dark winter night. He'd brought an armload of blankets, a thermos of hot chocolate, and a picnic basket loaded with sandwiches, oranges, and peppermint bark.

What girl wouldn't be impressed? I'd begun to relax in this winter-wonderland date he'd created, and my insides muddled at his charm, like they had the first day we'd met. But then he had thrown those two words out, siphoning away the magic of suspended reality.

"Joe, yes." I gripped my warm mug with both palms. "What about him?"

"He stayed with Sydney tonight?"

I chuckled. "Since you already know the answer, that's not really a question."

Craig ducked away, his shoulders rolling forward as he leaned both elbows against his knees. "No, I guess it's not. But I'm wondering if there's something between you two?"

I fingered the edge of the quilt draped over my shoulders. "Define *something*."

"You seem...uh...close."

"We've been good friends for a long time." I tried to cut the hard edge from my voice. Not sure I was successful. "He's been around since Sydney's accident and has been her physical therapist from the beginning, so, yeah. We're close."

"But not..."

"We've never dated."

"Why not?"

Did he have the right to ask these questions? *Because Joe never asked...*I thought. In the space of silence, I mulled over that answer. It was the only reason I could think of, and that fact bothered me.

"I'm sorry." Craig sighed and then turned a direct look on me. "That's really putting you on the spot. It's just that you kind of exploded on him the other day at school, and he handled it, and then at the parade you two seemed to have worked it out fine and are...uh, good again. I guess. Takes a pretty strong relationship to do that, you know? Just made me wonder if I'm trying to step into a spot that's already taken."

I bit the inside of my bottom lip, trying to shield my heart from Craig's observation. It wasn't helping the whole confusion thing going on in there. But I couldn't block out what he'd said, and I didn't know exactly how to answer him.

"I guess that maybe we have a unique friendship," I began, staring into the flames, considering the afternoon that had just passed. Joe stayed with Syd and me at my parents'—he'd determined Dad had sprained his knee but didn't need to make the trip to urgent care, and then stayed for Sunday dinner. My mom's doing. "He's walked with me through some pretty tough times—with Syd and then with my dad's accident." I drew a breath and forced my gaze to Craig. "But there hasn't been anyone in that spot you're talking about for quite a while. I just haven't been ready for it yet."

Craig held an unwavering look on me: open, trusting, and sincere. "Are you ready now?"

Words didn't immediately form in my head. I set my mug on the arm of the chair and fidgeted, grasping for an answer I didn't have.

Craig reached over and covered my knee with his hand. "Not a question you were expecting on a first date, right?"

A bundle of air escaped from my lungs, a sort of laugh of relief. "Not really." I covered his hand with my own, and the tingles I'd been missing returned with a million little buddies fluttering through my veins. "I'm glad to be here with you tonight though. Is that an acceptable answer?"

His hand turned, and his fingers wove through mine. "Definitely." He raised my knuckles and brushed them across his lips. "I'm glad too."

***

It was funny that as a teenager I thought a curfew was the dumbest, most childish expectation adults had for their kids. Now an adult myself, home by ten made more sense than the *wing it and pay for your stupidity in the morning* policy.

Craig dropped me off at 10:03.

"Thanks for the bonfire," I said as he shifted his car into park. "I wasn't sure how you'd pull off a date on a Sunday night around here."

The dome light allowed me to see his grin. "Are you impressed?"

"Very."

"Mission accomplished." He leaned over and brushed a light kiss across my cheekbone. The roughness of his jawline scraped across my skin as he pulled back to look into my eyes. He paused, waiting...

I didn't close the gap, even though I knew he'd given me a silent invitation. Those blue eyes examined my face, searched my eyes, his mouth hovering near for two more breaths, and then he leaned away.

My pulse sputtered, and heat filled my face. I wasn't any good at this, and I couldn't understand my heart or my actions. Maybe I wasn't ready to date again.

"My week's pretty loaded at the school." Craig's finger traced over my hand. "But I'd like to see you again, if it's okay."

"I'd like that." Maybe by the next time I'd have myself figured out.

"Friday night?"

"Definitely."

He curled a gentle hold over the hand he'd been fingering. "Good. It's a date."

Not risking eye contact would have been beyond rude, so I did. My heart went a little gooey at the warmth in his smile.

"Yes, it is."

After one last brush of his mouth over my knuckles, he released my hand, and I exited the car. I kind of thought he'd walk me to the door—he was that kind of guy—but relief sagged through me when he didn't. How terribly uncomfortable would it have been for Joe to have met us there? Not that I'd expected that of Joe, but still.

So I made it up the short walk on my own, his headlights illuminating the way. Craig didn't back down from my drive until I was safely through the door, a sign that he was actually a gentleman and probably had the same tug of anxiety about Joe being in my house. After all, Craig hadn't sat with me in church so that I could avoid a scene. The man was exceptionally thoughtful.

Which made the tug-of-war in my chest nearly inexplicable.

Joe didn't meet me at the door. I was in my kitchen, just to the left of the entryway, before I spotted him. Reclined on my small, used, and mostly uncomfortable sofa, his sock-covered feet were propped up on the pallet coffee table he'd helped me manufacture two years before. With a book folded open on his chest, the man was sleeping.

I dropped my keys in the bowl I kept on the counter for such things, slid my heavy coat from my shoulders, and walked toward him, dumping the parka on a dining chair at my small round table.

"Joe," I whispered.

One silent breath in. One whispered breath out. He didn't stir.

I stopped at the arm of the sofa and leaned against it. There was something about watching a man sleep...

Starting with his dark, straight hair, my eyes traced over the details of Joe White. His forehead sloped gently to meet the dark eyebrows that framed those kind coffee-colored eyes, which were shut. Dark lashes rested against his cheeks, contrasting against his winter-white skin. Just below, though, the pale skin faded under the dark, closely trimmed beard he kept year round.

My fingers itched to trace that rough jawline, and I suddenly wondered how I had missed how handsome Joe really was.

That wasn't it. I hadn't missed it. I'd thought about it when Jane suggested he was the mystery Santa leaving a gift on my front porch. But knowing a man was good looking and being attracted to that man...wasn't the same thing.

Without permission, my attention strayed to his mouth. Tension tugged in my chest. Up until that week, I'd never wondered...

But there I was, staring at my sleeping, *very* attractive friend, wondering.

With a sudden breath in, Joe's eyes fluttered open. I couldn't move, despite knowing how strange it must be for him to wake up to a woman sitting nearby, staring.

He stared back, and for a moment something I'd never seen in his expression passed through his gaze. Soft. Then intense. Almost...intimate.

That tension near my heart spiraled to my stomach, sending a mess of butterflies fluttering throughout my core.

And then the moment was gone.

Joe's eyes cleared, and he sat forward, catching the book as it slid from his chest. "Hey. Sorry. Didn't mean to fall asleep."

"That's okay." I struggled to contain the mass of tingles still exploding inside me. "I just got in."

"Yeah?" He stood, arched his back in a stretch. "How was it?"

Those fluttery tingles died where they were, like tiny bubbles that all popped in unison. I didn't like the empty feeling they left behind. I looked down at my hands. "Okay. I mean good. It was good."

The space between us held in silence, and I felt his eyes on me. When I looked up, I found a shadow of that same intense look that he'd blinked away moments before.

Come back. Locked in our gaze, I stood, silently begging to see what I thought I'd seen then.

Guarded now, Joe examined me, his eyebrows heavy and drawn inward.

"Are you going out with him again?"

I broke our connection, which made me want to cry. "Yes." My answer came out not much more than a hoarse whisper.

Although he didn't actually move, I felt him pull away. "Then it must have been good."

My heart rate spiked as I raised my face to again catch his look. "I don't really know what I'm doing, Joe." My voice caught on his name.

I watched as his Adam's apple bobbed, but he turned away just enough that I couldn't gauge his thoughts.

"Maybe you're just scared. That's understandable."

Terrified. But not completely for the reasons he was implying. "I can't afford another huge mistake." *Please,* I silently pleaded, *if you like me...*

"You won't, Kale." Joe stepped toward me, closing the tense space between us and pulling me into a hug. "You're a hardworking, smart, beautiful woman. You're always putting others ahead of yourself, making sure they're taken care of. I know you'll be just fine."

Shaking, I snaked both arms around him, anchoring my grip on his sweater. While his words were kind, more generous than true, they didn't cover the ache that suddenly began to throb. They weren't the words my heart had wanted to hear.

Chapter Eight

Jane didn't waste a second. "So..."

"What?" I shrugged out of my coat and, while feigning stupidity, walked toward the shelf holding our clean aprons. Actually, I wasn't playing dumb. There were a lot of questions that could follow that dangling conversation starter. I wasn't going to play pin the tail on the inquiry. Answering the wrong one could spell emotional disaster.

"Where to begin?" Jane grinned, bumping me with her shoulder. "Let's start with the mystery box. What was in it?"

"I don't know."

"Seriously?" She pulled away and looked at me like I'd grown gills and a tail. "How is that even possible?"

Because I'm scared to find out. Couldn't tell her that, so I kept it to myself. "I forgot about it."

"Now I know you're lying. There is no way on *earth* that you could have forgotten about a secret-Santa gift left on your front porch."

Touché. "Fine. I didn't forget, but I'm not sure I'm going to open it."

"What?" Jane's voice hit an octave that suited an opera

singer.

I bit the fat part of my tongue. How was it that I finally had a suitor, and a good-looking, gentlemanlike one at that, and I was scared to death to know what he'd left for me in a surprise gift?

Suspicion replaced the shock on Jane's face as she crossed her arms over her chest. "You know who it's from, don't you?"

Turning away, I walked toward the front of the shop, my hands whipping the apron strings into a bow at my waist. "I have a pretty good idea."

"It's Joe, isn't it?"

"Good grief, Jane." I snagged the large water pot for the Bunn drip maker and then scowled at her. "No. We already talked about that."

"Come on, really?"

"Really." With more force than necessary—because, dang it, why'd she have to bring him up?—I flicked the water spout on. The hard stream of cold spray rather reflected my sudden gush of not-so-happy emotion. "Joe and I have been friends for five years. Five. Years. Why would he all of the sudden, out of the snow-laden clouds, decide to do something so…"

"Romantic?" Jane scooped fresh coffee grounds into a large filter.

"Out of character."

"Not out of character at all. He's a thoughtful guy."

He was that. But not in a…*romantic* way. Not with me.

"Look at how devoted he is to Sydney. Not to mention your dad. And you? He comes into this shop every day. I don't know anyone who really likes hot chocolate that much. Coffee? Yes. Tea? Sometimes. Hot cocoa? Not a soul."

The water sloshed its way to the fill line, and I was obligated to shut off the stream. "Everyone's allowed a quirk or two."

"Okay, fine, Sherlock. Who do you think it was?"

I replaced the carafe, now drained and ready to receive black richness in its empty belly, and flicked the Bunn on. Spinning, I faced Jane, working up what I hoped was the appropriate amount of enthusiasm for this revelation.

Sad. Shouldn't have to work up something like that. "Craig Erikson."

"Craig Erikson? Mrs. Rustin's nephew?"

How'd she know that? "Yes. We went out this weekend. Twice. And his aunt only lives two doors down from me. I caught him shoveling her drive on Friday morning."

"So naturally he would have shoveled your drive the day before." Jane rolled her eyes. "Kale, had you ever even met him before this weekend?"

Was I allowed to plead the fifth? I reached for a clean, dry rag and moved to the sink. Warm water ran over my hand and the cloth before I looked back at Jane.

"No."

"Then why—"

"It wasn't Joe, okay? So it must have been Craig. Let it be."

Jane drew up straight, her eyes widening. I looked away, staring at the crumpled, soppy rag in my hand. Kind of resembled the way my insides felt, all saggy and misshapen and out of place.

Christmas was supposed to be a magical time of year. Gifts were supposed to bring joy. But there I was, feeling like a crumpled-up wet rag.

Footfalls scuffled behind me, and then Jane's hand wrapped around one of my shoulders. She squeezed, letting the silence speculate about the state of my emotions. I felt my chin quiver, and I clenched my jaw.

"Is he nice?" Jane's tone softened, as if she understood my inner turmoil.

"He's very nice." I glanced at her and then moved to wipe tables.

Jane took up another clean, wet cloth and moved to the opposite end of the small dining space. "I've heard he's quite good looking."

"You've heard correctly. Craig definitely draws the eye." I wondered, as I remembered his well-defined face, those merry blue eyes, and that killer smile, where the swoony feelings had gone. Was I really that wishy washy?

Give a girl a pearl, and she'd rather have a diamond. That wasn't entirely accurate. I didn't care much for either. I just wanted that look I'd seen last night coming from a pair of brown eyes rather than blue. Was it unfair to want my friend to fall in love with me?

It wasn't fair to either Craig or Joe. And a grown woman should know better.

For the rest of the day, my stomach felt queasy, and I couldn't think straight. The fact that Joe didn't come in at all added another quill of discomfort to my already sore heart. I'd made him feel awkward the night before, clinging to him as if desperate, nearly crying in his arms. Not only did I have to fight away the disappointment in myself for this irrational flip of my heart, but I'd managed to miff up our friendship in the process.

Joe was the steady, solid constant in my life, the one person I couldn't afford to lose. Which meant I needed to get my head on straight and start directing my heart.

All of this I scolded into myself for the early part of the day, but when Ms. Ruthie answered the phone shortly after lunch and then said it was for me, I couldn't box away the rising hope that I'd hear Joe on the other end of the line.

"Kale."

I tried to stave away disappointment. "Hi, Craig. How are you?"

"Uh, well, I was better about five minutes ago. Sydney's conked her head, and I think you'd better come down and take a look."

The nausea came on full force as my heart began to kick. "What happened?"

"She fell on the playground. Listen, I've gotta go—my class is coming in, but I told the office I'd call you. It's best if you just come check her out, okay? I'll call you later to see how she is."

He hung up before I could get another word in. My throat tight and my pulse racing, I clunked down the landline and went for the back room.

"What's wrong, Kale?" Ms. Ruthie trailed my heels.

"Syd's hurt. I'm sorry. I've got to go."

I was pretty sure she was good with that—it'd be out of character for Ms. Ruthie not to be shooing me out the door, concerned for my daughter, but I wasn't actually listening when I left, so I wasn't positive. Either way, I left, my mind conjuring up all sorts of images involving blood, an ambulance, and an unconscious daughter. So when I walked into the front office of the school and everything was all business as usual, I nearly lost it.

"Where's Syd?"

"Back here." Joe's calm voice tugged me to the nurse's office while the secretary smiled and pointed.

Not bothering with the check-in-and-wear-a-badge operating procedure, I turned and launched into the back room. Joe was squatting in front of Sydney, using his phone flashlight to check her eye response.

"Use only your eyes, and look to your right."

Syd complied.

"Good. Now tell me what twelve times twelve is."

She scowled, leaning toward him. "I don't know that, silly. We're still learning how to count."

Joe chuckled, patting her knee. "Right you are. Now say hi to your mom, and tell her that you're okay."

Sydney leaned back from Joe's space and looked up at me, a faint smile on her little angelic face. "Hi, Momster."

My heart righted itself, and though I could still hear ambulance sirens in my imagination, the ER images faded, and I lowered myself beside her on the cot. "Hey, Princess Hurry Up. What happened?"

Her look turned mildly sheepish. "I was playing tag with some kids, and I slipped."

"Tag?" I felt a scowl crinkling my forehead, and I looked from her to Joe. He simply raised his brows.

"Yes, Mom. Everyone plays tag, especially in the snow. It looked fun, so I played too."

"Syd…"

Joe's hand cupped my knee, and I caught his eye again. *Bubble child.* That was what he was thinking.

But I had these boundaries for her so she wouldn't get hurt, and this was proof…

"Everyone takes a spill. It's part of life." Joe's thumb brushed the outside of my knee. "She's okay. But if you want to take her home for the rest of the afternoon, that'd be understandable."

Aware—probably too much—of his hand still warm on my knee, I battled a toxic concoction of emotions. Irritated that once again my judgment had been overruled. Grateful that he was here. Relieved—so very relieved that Syd was okay. What was I supposed to do with all of this buildup inside me?

"Where's the school nurse?"

Joe lifted from his squatting position, his vacated touch leaving a cool, empty spot where it had only moments before been warm. "She's at the high school right now. You're stuck with my second-rate opinion."

"I never said that."

His eyes settled on me with a deliberate smirk. "I know."

What was that supposed to mean?

"Am I going home, Mom?"

"Yeah." Standing, I focused on her, since paying attention to Joe was tying me into convoluted knots. "Should we go get your things?"

"I got it." Sydney pushed away from the cot, stretching

herself as tall as her full height would allow. "I'm fine, and I can go get them by myself."

Two against one. Not even fair. I was the one called out of work because my kid conked her head. How had I ended up on the defense here?

Didn't matter, because Syd didn't wait for my answer. With as much determination as I'd ever seen from her, she moved out of the office and started toward the kindergarten wing without a backward glance.

My eyes slid shut, and my chest caved. Pulse throbbing, I couldn't fight the crash of mixed-up emotions that washed over me again.

A hand, warm and familiar, cupped my shoulder, rubbed my arm, and then circled around my back. In the next breath, I was tucked against Joe's chest.

"She's okay, Kale. I wouldn't tell you that if she wasn't."

I sagged against him, feeling the strong thud of his heartbeat against my temple. "How hard did she fall?"

"I don't know for sure. I wasn't out there."

Straightening, I pulled away just enough to look at him. "Where were you?"

After a long, slightly reprimanding look, Joe let his arm fall away. "I have other patients, Kale. I was with one of my fifth graders when the office called me to check on Sydney."

Oh yeah, right. Joe's world didn't actually revolve around me and my daughter. Even if I thought it should. Which meant that my irritation with him about *allowing* her to play tag was completely unfounded. Making me a jerk.

I swallowed, wondering how exactly I should apologize

to him. Yet again. Not able to completely raise my heated face to him, I peeked up to determine the volume of his frustration.

Soft coffee-colored eyes waited for mine. I melted. Heart and body. If I hadn't been standing in the school nurse's office, I would have stepped into his space, nuzzled against his chest, and wrapped him in my arms.

I wondered if he'd return the gesture.

Certainly he would have. But it wouldn't have meant the same thing to him. Probably. I couldn't afford the risk, and this time not just because of Sydney. The piercing ache of rejection left over from Brad had a way of surfacing in those kinds of moments.

So I returned my thoughts to neutral, common ground. "Syd's head..." I stepped back. "No concussion?"

"I don't think so, but it'd be a good idea to keep an eye on her the rest of the afternoon." He seemed to return to professional Joe White, his tone official and a little distant. "Maybe check on her a couple of times tonight, just to be safe."

Grappling for some kind of stability, and fighting away the disappointment at his switch, I nodded.

Sydney reappeared in the office, her pack slung over her shoulder, and Craig Erikson in tow.

His hand dropped to her shoulder. "She's headed out, huh?"

"Yeah, I'm going to take her home." I focused on the blue eyes saturated with concern. "Thanks for calling me."

"Not to the doctor?"

"No. Joe thinks she's okay. We'll just go home and take it easy."

Craig's look slid from me to the man standing behind me, a slight quirk raising his brow. "Are you—"

"Kale's a good mom. She can make her own decisions." He stepped from behind me and moved toward the office door. "I've got to finish up here and get to a couple other patients in town before the game tonight. Call me if you have questions, Kale."

He didn't wait for me to respond. Didn't even give me another glance as he walked away.

The sight of his back rounding the corner before disappearing into a side hall stayed with me. Somehow it cracked my heart—as if it meant more than his simply going back to work.

Things between us had changed. He wasn't coming back.

***

The smell of take-'n'-bake pizza from a grocery freezer still clung to the air as I piled two used plates into my kitchen sink. Before I flicked on the faucet, my phone chimed against the counter.

How's Syd?

I looked at the text, glancing back to the sender as if perhaps rechecking the name would make it change.

Joe had a couple of home visits and a basketball game to work that night. I shouldn't have expected that he'd check on us. But having Craig ask rather than Joe seemed like a cold slap of hard reality.

And there it was—reality. Craig was interested in me, and why the heck wasn't I completely smitten with that fact? I'd never guessed a camera-ready-at-any-moment man would cast a glance at me all on my own. Add in single mom who didn't have a whole lot going for her, and I should have just been face-down grateful.

And he was nice. Really great, actually. What on earth was wrong with me?

You just want what you can't have. Foolish woman.

That had to be it, because things hadn't gone complicated between Joe and me until I'd decided *Joe and me* should actually be a thing.

It was Jane's fault. That was the only explanation. I would have never put my thoughts in that direction if she hadn't put his name out there as the possible secret Santa.

Thanks for that, my dear friend.

Forget it. All of it. There was a handsome blue-eyed man, who happened to be amazing with kids and tons of fun besides, waiting for me to text him back. Operation Fall For Mr. Right commenced. Leaving my sink, along with the waiting dishes, I wandered into the living room, phone in hand.

She's fine. Just a small headache, but nothing loopy. Thank you for asking.

Send. Operation in full swing.

I settled on the sofa, where my girl was coloring, and brushed a finger over the egg knot on her head. Not wanting to undermine Joe's opinion, I refrained from calling urgent care when that lump summoned all kinds of worry. I looked it up on WebMD, which I was pretty sure would not set well with Joe either. But he wouldn't have to know about that.

Swelling *out* was actually a good sign. Swelling *in* would be bad. Guess the Internet agreed with Joe.

The text chime on my phone dinged again. Craig had responded.

Sure. Will she be in school tomorrow?

A small grin pulled on my mouth. *Yes.*

Crag texted again. *Relieved.*

Yeah, me too. Another ding followed.

We still on for Friday?

Operation procedure check. *Yeah. Looking forward to it.*

Which reminded me. I needed to talk to my mom about keeping Syd. No way was I going to let Joe stay with her again.

Operation snag.

I'm not thinking about Joe right now.

Operation righted.

The chime sounded one more time. *Me too. Good night, Kale.*

That was abrupt.

What had I expected? That he'd offer to come over, hang out?

Would have been nice...and helped the operation move forward.

The man has a job...

I tucked my phone away on the side table and snuggled Sydney into my arms. She stopped her coloring and burrowed against me.

"I'm sorry I got hurt today, Mom."

Pressing a kiss to the top of her head, I pulled her tighter. "You don't need to be sorry. I feel bad for you though."

"You don't like me playing those kinds of games though."

Bubble kid. Nice poke into the conscience. I drew in a long breath and let it out slowly. "Do you ever feel afraid, Syd?"

She wiggled to look up at me. "I feel afraid when they stick an IV needle in my arm. I don't like it."

Words not spoken by very many little girls. "But you do it. You never even cry."

"I know. Because you told me once that we need to be brave to get better."

I said that? Must have been the alter-ego me. Didn't sound like fear-laden, wrap-the-kid-in-cotton me.

"Well, I need to work on being brave, letting you take on more of life. I kind of hold you back."

Sydney pulled away from me completely. "You just love me, Mom-ster. That's okay."

"I do love you. But sometimes I need to let you go a little more so that you can live. I let fear make my decisions, and that's not really a good thing."

"Joe says that there's nothing wrong with *feeling* afraid. The thing to remember is that we don't have to bow to the fear."

I studied her, trying to push away the fact that she gained so much from a man I was trying not to think about.

"When did Joe tell you that?"

Her little shoulders curled in, and she looked at her

hands.

"Syd?"

"He just says stuff like that sometimes." She looked up and flashed me one of her brave-face smiles, which meant that she wasn't going into it.

Were mothers supposed to allow their children to keep some things to themselves? I wanted to prod this little mystery out of her, but something small yet powerful told me to let her have her space. Overcoming my overbearing impulse to interfere took an enormous amount of self-discipline. But I managed.

"How about a movie before bed?"

Her real smile surfaced. "On a school night?"

"Just this once." I ran a hand over her dark silky hair. "Go pick it out."

Of course she would pick the one Pixar movie that had ever made me cry. *Inside Out* it was. As if I hadn't had enough emotions for the day.

After the credits began to roll, we shut the TV off, and Sydney dutifully brushed her teeth and climbed into bed. On my knees bedside her mattress, I gathered her hands in mine, and we prayed.

"Jesus, thank You that You are my friend," she began, her usual opening, "and that You can make me brave. Thank You my head is okay, and for Joe being there today. Thank You for Mom-ster. Please help her feel brave too. Amen."

Kids didn't flower their words, you know? Just said it and kept it real. So I followed her lead.

"Jesus, thank You for loving us. Thanks for keeping Syd safe today. Thanks for Joe. Please help me to be brave. Amen."

I kissed her, shut off her lights, and paused at the door. "Good night, Princess. I'll check on you in a while, okay?"

"Okay. But I'm fine."

I smiled, blew a kiss, and left her room. In the kitchen, I glanced at the digital clock on the oven. Nine thirty.

Such an awesome mom. Let my kid stay up and watch a movie until nine thirty on a Monday night.

I glanced at the dishes still waiting for me to wash. Tomato sauce from the frozen pizza I'd served for dinner was smeared on Syd's plastic plate.

I needed to get rid of that. Carcinogens. Or something like that. I'd read about them in a parenting magazine somewhere. But Syd loved that *Cars* plate.

My heart spiraled downward.

Pizza. I fed my daughter *frozen pizza* for dinner. I should be cooking good-for-you meals, free of all those letters that were apparently bad for you. I didn't know what they were or what they stood for, but I read about them somewhere on some blog.

And the apples I'd sliced...I hadn't sprung for organic, because fruit is expensive in December.

What was I feeding my kid?

Such a failure.

Scrubbing my hands over my face, I slipped into misery. *I am trying, God...*

I wondered, as I began to fill my sink with warm water and suds, if He was looking down on me, shaking His head.

Great. The guilt voice had already started, and I hadn't even changed into my pj's. Given the fact that I was still worried sick about Syd's head—why hadn't I taken her into the clinic? Joe could have been wrong. After all, he was a physical therapist, not a doctor—I figured sleep was going to be a wash that night. Good way to start the week.

With my eyes stinging, I ran a clean washrag over the used plates, forks, and cups and then rinsed them all with water hot enough to slough the skin off my fingers. I wondered, while towel drying them and replacing them in the cabinets, what my little emotion characters looked like and who was at the central control board.

Guilt.

Yeah, him. After hanging the dish towel to dry, I slid onto the sofa and fingered the movie cover. How come Joy didn't take over on my switchboard? Why Guilt?

I knew why. I'd made a hash out of my life. Stupid, stubborn choices. Purity before marriage? Thought that was archaic. Dumb. And mostly, I had a powerful longing pretty much my whole life to be noticed, to be loved. That seemed inexplicable. My family loved me, but it didn't satisfy. I even knew Jesus loved me, but that wasn't the same thing as the romance I craved.

So when Brad pushed for more physical intimacy, I gave it. I wanted to. When he suggested we live together, in my mind that had one course. We'd move in, find out if it worked, get married, and live happily ever after. So we were pregnant. That didn't throw that plan off. The course of my life seemed charted quite nicely. Take that, you old-and-not-relevant religious standards.

And then everything came unraveled. It was all my

fault.

The *if onlys* and the *I should haves* had been mildly stayed by the fact that Sydney was, despite how everything came about, the best thing in my life. I could focus on that in the daylight hours when her laughter and her stout determination lent me happiness, or when her hand would slip into mine and everything in my world calmed and felt right. But at night...

Guilt. What if I ruined her life the same way I'd taken my own south?

There were so many ways to screw it all up.

I could imagine being brought before God in heaven someday. He'd look at me, one eyebrow cocked, and say, "Well, Kale, you made it. Just barely—and only thanks to my Son. But let me show you all of the ways you could have done better." He'd flick open a scroll, and it would continue unrolling, exposing an endless list of failures as it flipped down the long aisle and out the door.

Sitting there with that scene playing out in my head, I wilted. My shoulders curved inward, and I tucked my knees up against my chest, resting my forehead against them.

"I'm sorry, God," I whispered. "Please show me how to do better. How can I find favor in your eyes? I want to. I just keep messing up."

Tears dripped from my eyelids, landing on my jeans.

I wasn't sure how long I sat like that, heaviness draped over me like an iron blanket. It must have been a while, because when a soft knock sounded from my front door,

I felt stiff as I unfolded from my fetal position.

Nearly ten o'clock, I hesitated before I answered. In fact, another quieter knock sounded before I pulled it open.

Joe stood on the front porch, his head tilted to look into the slivered opening I'd allowed.

"Hey. I figured you'd still be up. Was I wrong?"

I tugged the door open the rest of the way. "No, you were right." He passed in front of me into my house, and I shut the door. "What are you doing?"

He pushed his hands into his coat pocket and shrugged. "The game just ended, and I kind of guessed you'd be worrying about Syd, so I thought I'd stop and check on her." He paused, studying me in a way that seemed intimate. One hand came from his pocket, and as he stepped forward, his thumb traced a line over my cheek. "You've been crying."

The old hunger for touch spilled through my mind, and for a breath I leaned into the hand near my face. He didn't pull it away.

What if...

I shut my eyes and reminded myself how much Syd and I needed this man. Standing up straight, I pulled away from his touch and looked at my feet.

"Just tired. Nothing to worry about."

His hand went back into his pocket. "Then why aren't you sleeping?"

I whipped my attention back to him, ready with a sassy reply about him being there. It died in my throat the moment his intense stare sank into me.

"You know I can't."

He nodded. "Shall I check on her?"

"Well," I sighed. "She just went to sleep about thirty minutes ago." My shoulders drooped as I stepped toward the sofa I'd just vacated.

Joe followed me, settling into the chair nearby, his look still pinned on me. "You act like that's a crime."

"Nice parenting, right? Let my kid stay up late to watch a movie after she bonked her head, when she's got to get up for school in the morning."

He glanced at the movie case on the pallet table between us and then looked back at me. "Is that why you're upset?"

A lump the size of a softball ballooned in my throat.

"Kale, you're a great mom."

Yeah, he totally thought that. Especially with the way I didn't push her so that she'd be further along in her recovery process, and the fact that I bubble wrapped her with all my fears.

He reached across the space between us and gripped my hand.

I couldn't handle the storm anymore. "Stop it, Joe. I know that's not what you think." With a hard flick, I pushed his hand away.

"What?"

"She's behind in everything. She can't run, can't skip, can't even play tag without getting hurt. And you know what else? She's barely reading at grade level. I didn't work with her enough, and now she's behind."

"She spent half her young life in a hospital and on pain meds, Kale. She's fine. And she's only in kindergarten.

Did you expect her to read Dickens by Christmas?"

"Funny, Joe. You know I'm right. She's a whole year older than most of her classmates, and they came into school already knowing how to read. Do you know what it's like to see parents put up their brag posts about how awesome their kids are doing in school, knowing mine is sorely behind?"

Joe stood, took two steps, and sat down next to me on the sofa. "I don't even know what you're talking about. Syd is—"

"And she'll probably end up with cancer, thanks to her mother who can't seem to cook real food. I'm sure she'll thank me for that."

Slack-jawed, Joe just stared.

"Oh, and guess what else? I found out the other day that it's highly possible that all the meds she's been on in her life will likely affect her mental and emotional development. Isn't that great?"

"Where are you getting all this?"

I folded my legs in, returning to the position I'd been in before Joe showed up, and burrowed my head into the couch. His stare pierced me, but I couldn't look at him. Not after that crazy outburst.

The cushions beside me shifted, and his hand curved over my head, following the length of my lifeless brown hair. The next thing I knew, I was pulled tight against him.

"Stop reading that junk, Kale." His hand drifted down my back and up again, and then his fingers tenderly kneaded the tension in my neck. "Stop listening to the voices that pound you with defeat. You do the best you can with what you've got, and I think you're doing amazingly well."

A tremor shuddered through me, and then the dam completely burst. Tears I hadn't shed in a couple of years poured from my eyes. "I'm not what she needs."

One breathy chuckle escaped from his chest. "You love her. Put her ahead of yourself time and time again. You show her how to be kind and how to think about others. And she's awesome. Ask anyone. Her teachers adore her. The doctors think she's one funny, tough, incredible kid. I happen to love her like—" His voice cut off, and his hold loosened. Silence drifted between us, and I felt him emotionally pulling away from me again.

Why did he do that? Because he loved my daughter, but he couldn't feel the same for me? Was there any way that could change?

I looked up at him, the questions nearly flying from my tongue. He met my gaze, but the distance and resolution in his eyes kept my words caged.

Pulling away, his hand paused near my hair, and though he seemed to weigh his actions, he cradled the side of my head. "God has given you everything you need for life and godliness." A weighty pause settled between us, and his fingers curled into my hair. "Choose which voice to listen to, Kale. Conviction of sin comes from God, firm and clear. Guilt simply eats away joy with clouded accusations. You're not going to earn extra favor from God by trying to be someone else's version of the perfect mom. You'll only end up living in defeat."

Chapter Nine

The gentle memory of Joe's hand in my hair lasted through the night, and remnants of it greeted me in the morning. More than that, his words had buried into my heart. *Choose which voice to listen to.*

My morning coffee in hand, that advice propelled me to open my Bible, which, I have to admit, was not a common morning practice in my world. I knew better. It should be. But...

Always a *but*. But this was a new day, and I could choose to listen to God this morning rather than flying around fretting about everything I might be doing wrong. Pretty sure Joe had been quoting a verse the night before, I Googled part of it on my phone and slid onto a kitchen chair while I waited for the results.

The search sent me to 2 Peter 1:3, and I sipped my coffee as I flipped to the correct page in my Bible.

His divine power has given us everything we need for a godly life through our knowledge of him who called us by his own glory and goodness.

I continued reading, finding a list of things that I should be focused on rather than all of the other "lists" I've found in magazines and blogs. Things like goodness, and knowledge, and self-control, and perseverance, and godliness, and kindness, and love.

There was nothing in that about test scores, health checks, or running aptitudes. With those thoughts came a clear dawning...everything I'd tortured myself about were things that weren't priority to God. Good things, maybe, but not His focus. He focused on the heart, on things that lasted.

I'd been seeking badges of honor when I should have been prioritizing touches of grace.

Mind blowing to me, and even more so was the fact that as I let that realization sink in, I suddenly felt free. The voices of failure faded, and I felt a gentle smile beckoning me forward into fellowship with God.

He had *granted* me the ability to do these things. Me. The mixed-up young woman who ended up as a single mom. Me—with all my failures. Me—with my ordinary, complicated little life.

Who was I that He should *grant* me that kind of favor?

My bottom lip quivered. I was His.

"I am Yours," I whispered to the empty space. Tears spilled onto my cheeks. "Thank You. Thank You. Thank You..."

Something fresh and new started that morning. Freedom.

I never wanted to go back.

***

Life sort of evened out for the next couple of days. Sydney avoided injury, and I avoided voices of defeat. A fresh lightness lifted my spirit, and I continued reading the Bible in the mornings. I'd even stopped by the church on the way to my parents' house Wednesday afternoon, picking up one of those small paperback devotionals Joe carried with him to the coffee shop.

There was some good stuff in there.

My visit with Mom and Dad was, as always, bittersweet. As I unloaded the bag of groceries I'd brought, placing cold items in the fridge and pantry items in the cabinets, Mom told me about Dad's rough start to the week, which had kicked off with the fall he'd taken on Sunday. Joe had stopped by yesterday, even though Tuesday was not Dad's PT day. Said he wanted to check on the swelling and would adjust some of their weekly exercises.

Typical Joe White move.

Dad was stiff and sore, so Joe spent a good hour helping him stretch, talking with him while he iced, and just being their superhero.

I wanted that superhero.

These thoughts...they just persisted. *Ignore them.* Which meant that nothing was going to happen between me and Craig. It wasn't fair of me to push it when I knew good and well my thoughts and longings didn't pull toward him.

I needed to tell him.

That night after I tucked Sydney into bed, I spent quite a long while, in the silence of my house, praying over that. Craig was such a nice guy, and I had no business messing with his life—even if his interest was casual at this point, I didn't want to walk down that kind of dead-end trail. But I wasn't sure when or how to tell him.

God, do I keep our date Friday night? Cancel by a text?

Worry creeped its way into my thoughts. It'd be easier just to text him a quick message. *Can't make Friday night. Sorry. This just isn't going to work.*

Easier. And cowardly.

Please help me to be brave...

I eyed the package sitting on my counter, still unopened. Perhaps I should return it to him. After all, that was what started this whole thing. Maybe that was how it should end.

***

The next morning, with my coffee half gone, I finished reading about how God loved to give good things to His people, even when it seemed like only the hard stuff was coming our way, and my attention drifted back to the brown paper package. It sat in the middle of the table, just above my Bible and devotional.

I'd been so delighted to receive whatever was in that box. Just because it meant someone noticed me. It had almost felt like a whisper from God, that He noticed me too. For that reason, I was really struggling with the idea of returning it that night.

Fingering the burlap knot, I closed my eyes. *Please show me what to do...*

"Mom-ster, are you ever going to open that thing?"

Opening my eyes, I watched while my ornery little princess plopped herself onto the chair next to mine.

I chuckled. "I don't know."

"Why not?"

"Well, I don't know who it's from."

Her mouth twisted, disapproving. "How are you going to find out if you don't open it?"

I froze, staring at her.

"There's probably a card or a note or something inside."

Hadn't thought of that.

Shaking her head, she laughed. "You're a silly, Mom. Just open it."

"You think I should?"

"Someone gave it to you to have." She stood, leaned into my side, and patted my shoulder. "You have to receive a gift in order to have it, you know."

Apparently she listened during Sunday school.

My fingers twitched, and I tugged the small package toward me.

Sydney leaned closer, whispering in my ear. "Open, open, open..."

"Okay." I laughed. "Go get some breakfast, little pest."

She went for the cereal bowls, and I loosened the knot. Hope and anxiety played tug of war. I didn't know what I was hoping for, but I was sure I wouldn't want to give whatever it was back.

Flipping the gift, I picked at the packing tape until the seams parted. The brown paper fell away, and I was holding a silver metal snowflake with a white ribbon at the top.

A Christmas decoration?

Gotta admit, the anticipation kind of deflated.

Sydney came back, carrying her full bowl between her hands and carefully setting it onto the table before she plunked back onto her chair.

"Oh, that's pretty. Who's it from?"

"Doesn't say. Maybe it was for you?"

She shook her head, looking at me like I was

ridiculous. "Why would anyone want to play secret Santa with me? I have Christmas parties at school and church, so there's no point. Plus, that thing is way too nice for some kid to buy."

I lifted the ornament from the felt box, the cool of the metal seeping into my palm. It was heavy and well crafted. Syd had a point.

But still...a Christmas ornament?

Maybe this had all been Jane. She was messing with me.

No. Jane wasn't that mean.

Replacing the snowflake in its rather posh-looking box, I sighed. No answers. That left me still wondering if I should return it tonight. Would that be adding insult to injury? Craig was a grown man. He'd probably handle it just fine, but it still seemed...ungrateful.

"I like it, Mom-ster," Sydney said around a mouthful of Cheerios. "I think you should hang it in the window."

"That might look pretty." I pushed to my feet and moved to set my mug in the sink.

"Yeah, and we can remember that we're special whenever we look at it."

Say huh? I lifted an eyebrow at her. "We can?"

"Yeah, like Joe says."

Joe said what?

She paused, looking at me like I was struggling with two plus two. Joe was right. She was a very smart kid. I shouldn't have been so worried.

"There is no such thing as an ordinary snowflake. Joe showed me the other night. We took a piece of black construction paper outside, and he showed me how God makes each one different. Unicreak."

"Unique?"

"Yeah, that's it. Unique. And we're like that. God makes us each special and loves us especially."

Pretty sure that wasn't exactly what Joe had said, but...

My heart puddled, and I didn't want to return the gift at all. What if Joe had—

Was that even possible? He hadn't said anything. Not one single word. And he'd babysat for me so I could go out with another man. And the snow shoveling?

No. I was sure that was Craig. I had virtual proof.

"Mom-ster, are you still here?"

"Yep." I startled, refocusing on her.

"Are you going to hang it in the window?"

My heart squeezed and then started to throb. I didn't know anything for sure. Except that we were going to be late yet again if we didn't get after it. Snowflakes could wait. I had a life to live.

***

"Did you open it yet?"

Jane had refrained from asking the entire week, but she apparently couldn't hold her curiosity in any longer.

I rolled my eyes at her and then grinned. "I did. This morning."

Cheerleader energy bubbled out of her. "And..."

"It was an ornament. A snowflake."

Cheerleader energy fizzled. "A snowflake? Oh." Her shoulders slumped in. "I was sure..."

"Sure what?"

Tossing her ponytail, she straightened her shoulders. "Well, you're right then. It definitely wasn't Joe. He knows you're not a winter fan. Why would he give a girl who always longs for the beach a snowflake? Doesn't make any sense."

My chest deflated, as if she'd just murdered the last of my wispy hope.

"Man, though, I just thought..."

Pinned to the floor, I stared at her. "What? What did you think?"

"Well, he hasn't come in all week, and with you seeing that other guy, I was pretty sure that math was easy. But it must have been a coincidence. Craig wouldn't have any way of knowing you're not really into snow, so I guess you were right all along. That's a relief, right? No triangles to straighten out."

Relief didn't even pull a faint tug on my heart. Pounding, it grasped a death lock onto hope, irrational as it might be.

Joe giving me a snowflake didn't make much sense— Jane was right about that. But I didn't care. I wanted it to be him.

***

Craig wouldn't hear of meeting me at Ms. May's for dinner that night, which made everything about what needed to happen all the more uncomfortable.

Jane's logic had chased around in my brain all day, and I very nearly accepted that she'd been right about Joe *not* giving me the snowflake. That triggered vulnerability again, and I questioned the wisdom of breaking things off with Craig before I really gave it a chance to start.

Jennifer Rodewald

Maybe with some time, he'd take up more real estate in my mind and Joe would take up less, and things would work out.

I didn't want that. That was the hard truth. And playing that game with Craig simply wasn't fair.

"Tell me more about this job you've managed to create," I asked, pushing around a turkey pot pie and avoiding the topic I really needed to bring up.

Craig wiped his mouth and smiled. "Not much more to tell, really. I'm a traveling music-education child entertainer. Throw in some crafts, nature studies, and you have it about covered."

"Why traveling?"

Chuckling, he turned a quiet tone of red. "No one can justify hiring a live Mr. Rogers full time. But they don't want me to go away either. I would love to say I could do it for free, but there is that whole life thing."

"Yeah, that. It does demand some funds."

"Right." He leaned back, folding his arms over his chest. "It's all good though. I like it this way."

Clarity began to unveil itself. This wouldn't have worked, even without the whole Joe puzzle in the mix. Craig's calling didn't parallel my life. I was sure that if Craig and I were meant to be, we'd figure a way to work it out, but as I sat there looking at his boyish, eager grin, peace settled in the place that had still been uncertain. He was living out what he needed to be doing. Syd and I didn't fit well into that picture.

It was tempting to use that as the excuse in the *you and I aren't going to work* speech I was assembling in my mind. I wondered if that was a cop-out.

Silence settled around us. Craig shifted in his chair,

leaning forward on his elbows against the table.

"You're thoughtful tonight."

"Yeah." I fiddled with the napkin on my leg. "Trying to figure some stuff out."

His gaze didn't waver, and the pleasantness around his lips remained, even as his expression deepened in thought. "Us. This. That's what you're thinking about, isn't it?"

Heat crept up my neck, and I broke eye contact. "Yes."

"And you're not convinced."

"Convinced that you're a great guy? Totally. You are. I don't see it working though, and I've got too much at stake in my life to take a risk like that."

"Dating is a risk. And I get it—especially with Syd. But you don't know if you don't try."

Staring at my plate, I began to drown in my ineptness. I did know. This *wasn't* going to work—and that wasn't his fault. But I didn't have the words or the courage to tell him why.

Drawing in a long breath, I looked back at him, praying he'd accept my flimsy answer. "Maybe I'm just not ready yet."

I could actually hear the ticking of his watch as the seconds scraped by. Craig continued studying me, and after a few breaths, his head moved from side to side. "I don't think that's it." One side of his mouth slid upward, an ironic expression given the words that followed. "I think I'm just not the guy."

My heart stalled as the heat flared into a full-on blaze,

and I looked for something to say in the depths of my dirty plate.

Nothing.

Craig's hand covered mine and squeezed. "It's okay, Kale. I can live with it—and I'd rather you be honest."

Swallowing, I chanced a peek at him. Still calm, pleasant. He'd sure be a catch, this nice, good-looking man. But not mine.

"So." He sat back, looking almost as if he'd just shrugged off the whole conversation we'd just muddled through. "Can a friend still buy a friend some gingerbread cake?"

My stomach squeezed painfully. "Can a friend ask for a rain check? I can't eat anymore."

Craig flashed that oh-so-mesmerizing smile. Except no butterflies for me. Or swooniness. I smiled back, and suddenly we were okay—I was okay.

"How about a snowflake check?"

Screech. Maybe not so much okay. Was that a hint? I should have brought the ornament—given it back to him.

One thick eyebrow hiked on his face. "You know, since it's winter out there and there's snow, not rain?"

"Uh...yeah."

He rubbed the back of his neck, the first nervous gesture I'd witnessed from him. "Okay, that was bad. I'll work on it. But yes, a rain check would be fine. Home?"

"I think so."

"You got it." He rose from his place, waited while I stood, and then pushed in my chair.

I dug around in my brain to find normal again.

Numbly following him, I slipped into a state of

unawareness while he stopped at the hostess desk. I think he paid, and I was such an idiot because I should have forked over my share, but my mind wasn't working on that.

I could give it back to him when he dropped me off at home. But that would mean I'd need to ask him to wait or invite him in. Wasn't that contradictory?

Had dating always been this complicated?

That wasn't right. We just cleared that up—Craig and I weren't dating. Friends. Friendships weren't this complicated. Unless it was my friendship with Joe we were talking about. But we weren't, and why was Joe in my head while I was on this nondate with Craig?

The man wouldn't leave me alone.

I snapped back to reality when the cold winter air blasted against my face. Craig took my elbow, and we double-timed it to his car. He opened my door. I dropped into the passenger's seat, and he came around to start the engine.

"Looks like more snow." He sucked air in through his teeth. "I'm supposed to be over in Cherry County Monday. Could be interesting."

"Always on the go." I looked at him, and he nodded. "I'm sorry if you stayed in town for this."

He smiled, flicking the heater knob to full blast. "I'd tell you that I'm not sorry, but I don't think that's going to make you feel any better. So I'll tell you that I'm hanging around to catch one more Rustin family dinner before I head out. I kind of love those gatherings."

Chuckling, I exhaled. "Good to know. That does make me feel better. And I can see why—the Rustins seem like quite a fun group."

"True that. And I'm glad you feel better—I don't want you to feel guilty." He'd put the gear into reverse but paused before he backed out of the space. "Promise, okay?"

Looking at him, I couldn't help a grin as he held a fist in midair between us. Clenching my right hand, I bumped his knuckles, knowing exactly why the kids and the teachers alike thought this man was amazing.

"You'll do well, Craig Erikson. I'm glad God has called you to the work you do, because it's pretty incredible, and you're perfect for it."

"Don't know about that—mostly I have a ton of fun." He'd backed out, and we were moving forward toward my house. "But I do get to meet some pretty awesome people along the way."

He squeezed my shoulder, and I wondered why he'd insinuate awesomeness about *me*. People didn't come much more ordinary than me.

Chapter Ten

Craig had been right. It snowed again. A fresh six-inch layer had covered the already snowy ground by late Saturday afternoon. While Syd finished watching her allowance of one movie per Saturday, I stared at the flakes outside as they continued to drift to the ground.

My study lifted to the horizon. White, white, everywhere white.

But then the glint of silver hanging in the center windowpane to my right caught my attention.

There are no ordinary snowflakes.

Joe and Sydney, they were a pretty special pair. My heart did that painful-pleasure squeeze thing, when something hits you bittersweet, and I wondered why they'd been talking about snowflakes in the first place.

Sydney pushed a chair up to the window where I stood, climbed onto it, and looked outside.

I reached for her hand and squeezed it. "Is your movie done?"

"Yep."

"Did Elsa bring back summer?"

She laughed. "Always. Is that what you're wishing for

right now?"

"No." I hugged her close. "I was just thinking that it's kind of pretty—and amazing when you think about all those little flakes being unique."

"That's what Joe said."

Her head tucked against my shoulder, and she sagged against me contentedly. "I like the snow, Mom-ster."

"I know. I'm glad." I rested my head on top of hers and sighed. "You help me see life differently—did you know that, kiddo?"

"No."

"Well, you do. And I'm thankful."

She didn't answer, but squeezed my waist and snuggled in closer. For a few rare moments, she stayed still and quiet, and I savored such a treasure.

"Hey, Mom, is Joe going to sit with us at church tomorrow?"

And there he was again.

"I don't know. He usually does, so probably. Why?"

She shrugged, pulling away. "I miss him."

"Miss him? Don't you see him at school? Doesn't he come and do your therapy during your extra-help time?"

"Yeah, but he didn't hang around. He usually finds me at recess, and we play, but he didn't this week. And we didn't go to Grandma and Grandpa's while he was there on Friday. It just hasn't been the same, and that makes me sad. I miss him."

That bittersweet tug morphed into full-blown heartache. I had no idea what to say—what to do. So I hugged her again.

"Can I ask him?"

"Ask him what, Syd?"

She pulled away and looked up, her normally happy *let's take on life* face now pleading. "Can I ask him if he'll sit with us?"

I chuckled. "Of course, baby."

She studied me, questions lurking in her eyes. But instead of being her usual forthright self, she nodded, climbed off the chair, and took herself to her room.

I knew exactly what she wanted to know. Would Mr. Erikson be there too? It was tempting to tell her the truth, but that was sure to prompt more questions. Ones that involved Joe. Questions that tugged in my heart too.

But I didn't have any answers. At least, not answers I wanted to accept.

***

He did it again.

Coffee slopped out of my travel mug as I staggered to a sudden stop. My driveway had been shoveled clear. Again.

I glanced down the block, across the yard that separated mine from Mrs. Rustin's. Her driveway was also clean, piles of snow and faint tracks from a recent shoveling evident on her cement.

Guilt gnawed a fresh hole in my gut. This was too much.

"Mom, you said we were late. Let's go."

Princess Hurry Up had slept off her funk from the night before. Wished I had too. It seemed completely unfair that my late night involved quiet tears, when, if I had just been able to redirect my heart, I could have been basking in the glow of new possibilities with Mr.

Dreamy, who apparently liked to shovel.

Thanks, my stupid heart.

Attempting to bury irritation—with myself for being so foolish, with the guy down the street whose kindness suddenly turned frustrating, and with the man whose love for my daughter had captured my desire—I marched to the car and set out for church.

Conjuring up a Christmasy mood before we arrived was a failed mission. I was completely lost to Grinchiness. Blame it on lack of sleep, among other things. Glad for our tardiness, I followed Sydney into the sanctuary, down the right aisle and to the middle pew.

There he was. Mr. Dependable. Mr. Quietly Stole My Heart. Mr. We're Just Friends.

My heart shrank two sizes. Wasn't that the Grinch's problem? I didn't want to be there, singing Christmas hymns about joy and hope and happiness. I wanted a full pound of chocolate. About four cups of coffee. A sappy Hallmark Channel Special and a box of tissues. Anything but to sit with Sydney between Joe and me, the three of us looking exactly like what I wanted but couldn't have.

But I was stuck. As I lowered onto the pew, I glanced over, catching Joe's smile as he silently greeted Sydney, all genuine and happy. His eyes moved up to connect with mine, and the smile faded.

"Hey, Kale," he whispered.

"Hi."

The arm that he'd stretched behind Sydney fell away, and he spread his fingers against his jeaned thigh. Cool reserve drifted into his gaze just before he turned his attention to the pulpit.

I looked away, focusing on the music director up front.

My fingernails bit into my palm as a surge of hurt and anger nearly overwhelmed me.

Why did he do this? How did he not know what his indifference toward me did to my heart?

The music part of the morning passed, and Pastor taught again about God looking at and loving the ordinary people through Jesus.

Blinking, I buried my attention in the Bible I had opened on my lap. Not really seeing the words on the page or hearing much of what was being said, my heart turned upward and began to explode.

Do you see me? I'm doing the best I can...why am I such a mess? Did I do the wrong thing with Craig? And Joe...what am I supposed to do there? I need him in my life—Sydney needs him—but, God, I can't feel this way and not ache at his detachment...

The dam inside my mind burst, and my rant continued right on through the rest of the service.

"Mom, can I go say hi to Grandma?"

Sydney's voice jarred me. I looked up and glanced around. It was over. I'd spent the entire service whining to God. No, yelling at God.

"Mom?"

"Yeah." I shut my Bible. "Go on."

Syd virtually crawled over me and made her way to the back, where my mom stood talking with a small group of ladies. Which left me alone with the man who'd accidentally snared my tumbleweed heart.

Joe turned in the pew, angling himself to sort of face

me. "You okay this morning?"

"Yep." I refused to look at him. Gathering my things, I moved to escape.

His fingers brushed my arm, touching more my sweater than me. "Hang on. I wanted to talk to you about something."

Stuck. Again. I forced myself to glance at him. With softness and hesitation in his brown eyes, he met my gaze.

"Okay." I slid back against the bench.

Joe cleared his throat. "It's just that, well...I got something for Syd. For Christmas. I wanted to make sure it was okay with you that I gave it to her."

Weird. No one else bothered to ask something like that. I shrugged. "Sure. She said yesterday that you'd been busy and she missed seeing you, so she'd like that."

He looked down. "Okay. But actually, I was thinking maybe it'd be better if she didn't know it was from me. It might..."

I felt my eyebrows fold inward. "Might... What is it?"

He hesitated and then peeked back at me. "That new Lego Palace she's been talking about."

What? My eyes seemed to bulge out of my sockets as I stared at him. "Joe. That's too much. That thing costs a small fortune."

"I wanted her to have it." With his hand rubbing the back of his neck, he cleared his throat. "Look. Don't get mad, okay?"

"I'm not mad. That's just too generous. Why would you do that?"

After one deep breath, he settled that soft look back on me. "I know things are tight for you, and I know that with the snow and Sydney's accident at school, you haven't been getting the hours at the coffee shop you were hoping for. I just wanted to help, to make you"—he bit his lip and paused—"to make her happy."

I snagged onto the *you* part of that, and it felt like a barbed hook. *God, please...*

His hand moved through the space between us and rested on my shoulder. When he moved his thumb, brushing the spot near my neck, I felt it all the way to my toes.

"Okay?" he asked.

What were we talking about? I fought the temptation to lean into his touch by moving away from it. His hand dropped, falling back to his lap.

Sydney. Legos. That was what this was about. Not me, my heart wreckage, and my wishful thinking.

I'd wanted desperately to get her that set because it was the only thing she talked about when it came to her Christmas list. Truth was, I couldn't. Joe was right. I hadn't put in the hours I needed for that kind of gift to be feasible.

Having him give it to her triggered a storm of contradictions in me. Gratitude, frustration, jealousy.

That was my stuff though. Not Syd's.

"Yeah, that'd be okay. She'll love it."

Joe nodded and then shifted to stand.

I rose with him. "I think you should tell her who it's from though."

He glanced around the church, his inspection pausing

on Sydney at the back before moving toward the corner to the left. I followed his gaze until it landed on Craig.

"Nah. I think it's better as a Santa gift." He returned his attention to me, lifting a half smile. "Please?"

Not waiting for an answer, Joe pivoted and walked away, leaving me alone to muddle with that response.

I didn't feel up to wrestling with it, so I moved away too. Craig caught me as I reached the foyer of the building, a pleasant grin on his mouth, as always.

"You're still here." Forcing a smile, I stopped and faced him.

"Family dinner, remember? I'll head out this afternoon. Should be a good day for a drive."

In the pause, I nodded, and then I just couldn't stop myself. "Look, Craig. I know that you're probably just being the nice guy that you are, but you don't need to shovel my driveway. It kind of makes me feel guilty."

His smile faded as his eyebrows pulled down. Looking at me nearly sideways, his look bounced from me, out through the large glass doors, and back again.

"Kale, I think you've got me pinned with a little more credit than I deserve."

"What?"

"It wasn't me." He shoved his hands into his jeans pockets while he glanced back outside.

I followed his glance. Moving slowly next to one of his older patients, Joe was walking away from the building.

The moment Craig looked back at me, his grin resurfaced. With a wink, he reached for my arm and squeezed. "I'm just not the right guy."

My attention darted back to the man outside. Joe? He lived across town. Church was the opposite direction of my house from his place. Or the schools.

Joe did this? My heart spurted with wonder and joy, and happy adrenaline spilled through my veins. It had been him. The whole time it'd been—why didn't he say anything?

Slowly I peeked back at Craig. He eyed me with a smirk.

"I knew it." He laughed as he tugged me into a hug. "I'm taking notes from that guy. That was pretty smooth."

I didn't know what to say as he let me go.

"Go on, before he leaves. The past few days have probably been killing him."

Him? What about me? My face warm, I moved to give Craig one more hug. "I'm so sorry. I didn't know..."

Craig turned me to face the door and nudged me with a playful push. "Go. I'm fine."

That was great for him, but *fine* wasn't the word for me. I couldn't make my thoughts line up straight.

Didn't matter. By the time I'd collected Sydney, checked with my mom about their welfare and promised to come over the following afternoon, and then finally made it out the door, Joe had already left.

***

I stewed about it the rest of the afternoon. Wrote about twenty text messages and promptly deleted each one before my strung-out emotions let me push Send. Tried to distract myself by playing in the snow with Sydney. And stared at the snowflake dangling in my window.

I loved it.

While Sydney was in the shower, darkness draping the land outside, text number twenty-one left my thumbs.

I need to talk to you.

Send.

Great. I sent it.

What if he called me? I couldn't do this over the phone. Probably couldn't do this in person either. Texting was much better.

Come on, Joe. Text me back.

With my fist gripping it like it was my lifeline, I stared at the phone. After an eternity of probably thirty seconds, it chimed.

Everything okay?

No. I was a bundle of nervous energy, and now when it was nearly night and not logical at all, I'd decided I needed to see him. Now. That didn't seem *okay*.

We just need to talk. Please?

I heard the water shut off in the bathroom, and it suddenly dawned on me that I probably should have waited until Sydney went to bed.

A full minute passed. No response.

Terrific. *Now* he decided to put me off. Groaning at my phone, I set it on the counter and moved toward the bathroom.

"Syd?"

"Yeah?"

"Brush your teeth while you're in there, okay?"

"Yep."

I walked back to the kitchen and checked the phone. Nothing. Bless it.

Breathe, Kale. And stop acting like a trapped monkey.

What was he doing? Why didn't he answer?

"Mom, would you help me with my hair?"

Distraction. Thank you, Sydney. I went back to the bathroom, this time finding the door open. Sydney smelled like peppermint and vanilla. She'd gotten into the holiday soap.

Finger-combing her hair, I smiled at her in the mirror. "You smell like Christmas."

She clapped her hands. "I know! And guess what? Only one more week."

I chuckled and reached for the wide-tooth comb. After detangling the ends, I made long strokes, smoothing her thick dark hair. "Shall we braid it tonight?"

With a shrug, Syd agreed.

"Mom-ster, you're kind of off today. Are you okay?"

"Yep." Someday she'd figure out that way-too-quick answer was a cover-up. But not that night, and I was grateful. "So Christmas...what do you think will be under that tree?"

"I don't know, but I hope it's pink and white and green and has a lot of pieces."

Subtle, that girl. I could barely cap the excitement and joy that bubbled in my chest as I imagined her unwrapping the Lego Palace.

Thank you, Joe.

But, bless it, he could answer me already.

I secured her hair with a band, and we both exited the bathroom.

"Did you do your stretches yet?"

Her shoulders slumped, and she sighed. "It's like he's here..."

"You would love that." The words rushed out of my mouth before I thought them through. *I would love that.* Well, if things weren't all mixed up, and if he would only...

Sydney stopped her mopey progress down the hall and turned. Mischief lurked in her little face as she cocked her head. "Would you?"

Huh. How many people in this town had been speculating about Joe and me? My own daughter...

A knock at my front door interrupted that thought. I forgot how to breathe as I stood glued to the wood floor. Sydney gave me a *what is wrong with you* scowl and then moved past me to answer.

Joe was there. Now. Right that very moment when I didn't know what to say or do or anything.

"Hey there, Sydney. How are you?"

"Well." I imagined she punched her fists onto her hips. "There's a stranger standing outside our door."

"What?"

"Where have you been all week? I've been stuck playing tick-tac-toe with Colton, and I have to make myself lose just to keep it interesting."

"Oh-ho." Joe chuckled, and the sound of the door shutting clicked. "That is some sacrifice there, kiddo. I'd say I was proud of you, but I have a feeling you weren't all that gracious."

"Come on, Joe. Why have you been ditching me?"

Silence filled the room beyond my sight, and I wondered if Joe had squatted beside her or if he was running a hand over his head while he searched for an excuse.

"It was kind of a long week, buddy. I'm sorry."

Given the soft tone of his voice, I would have bet he was down at eye level with her.

"Syd, let it go, hon. He has a life." My heart quivered as I stepped around the corner. There he was, squatting next to her just like I thought he'd been. Mr. Dependable. Mr. Steady as He Goes.

Mr. Make My Knees Jell-O.

As Joe stood, he lifted an attempt at a smile, holding my eyes with those brown ones. Flecks of black peppered the irises, and I wondered how I hadn't noticed that before.

He broke the connection, glancing down to Syd and resting a hand on her wet hair. "Ready for bed, eh, buddy?"

"Yes." She reached up and took the hand on her hair into a grip. "I was just going to do my stretches."

"Good girl."

She grinned up at him, let go of his hand, and brushed past me. "See ya."

Joe's shoulders moved in a silent chuckle. But when his attention came back to me, he sobered.

"Everything okay, Kale?"

My chest hurt. "Yeah. We're fine."

He questioned me with a look.

Deep breath. *Just say it...*

"Did you shovel my walk this morning?" Oh dear. That came out sharper than I meant because I had to force it through the mass in my throat.

Joe drew back, his hand rubbing the top of his hair. "Well, uh. Um, yeah. I did." He squinted at me, stalling. Searching for an explanation, probably.

It'd been him...air caught in my chest. "And last week? That was you?"

Color stained the white skin above his dark beard. "Yes."

Without knowing it, I'd stepped closer, and a mere twelve inches of heated air separated us.

"I thought it'd be helpful." His hands moved to his pockets. "You're usually running late, and I just wanted..." He cleared his throat, glancing to the floor. "I just thought it'd help you out. I didn't mean to offend."

Offend? He'd mistaken my intensity.

"Joe."

Slowly his eyes rose back to me. There. *That* look—the one I'd seen when I startled him awake. It billowed in his expression, drawing me closer, stirring courage and that beautiful ache in my heart.

I stepped closer, lifting my hand until my fingers grazed the trimmed stubble on his jaw. "Please tell me the snowflake was you too."

His eyes slid shut as he leaned into my touch. "It was." His hand covered mine and then moved to slide over my hair. "I wanted you to know—maybe to see things a little differently."

"How?"

"You don't like winter—I know that, and that's okay. But maybe if you saw how amazing ordinary snow is, it wouldn't be so miserable. And maybe..." His voice wobbled. "...maybe you'd see yourself differently too."

No ordinary snowflakes. Joe was right—I'd looked for the hand of God in things that were special—in the things that seemed extraordinary. I'd been looking for Jesus in a palace, feeling like He was far off, when really, He came to the manger. He dwelt with the ordinary, and He usually poured out His extraordinary love in everyday ways. Through kindness and truth.

Blinking and a little shaky, I traced the curve of his bottom lip with my thumb. "Why didn't you say anything?"

His breath released in a single, soft laugh. "I wanted to. I had this ridiculous idea that I'd leave something for you every day until Christmas. The power of persuasion, I guess. But then you met Craig, and when I saw you with him, you seemed happy." He paused, his head tilting toward mine. "I want you to be happy."

That move toward me was irresistible, and with a small push on my toes and a hand on his chest to steady my quivering limbs, I brushed my lips against his. Not pulling more than two inches away, I whispered, "What if I said that you make me happy?"

He searched my face, heat in his look and intensity in his touch as he cradled my head within his gentle hands. When his eyes slid shut, his head lowered until it rested against mine, but he refused to rush the moment. His nose brushed mine, then slid against my cheekbone, down the side of my face, his lips nipping my jawline until they hovered oh so desirably above my own.

"Kale, I am in love with you."

I felt his words as his breath danced over my mouth. They washed over me with warm joy, settling into the waiting space of my heart. A perfect fit. No longer able to stand the remaining distance between us, I claimed his lips, and he tucked me close.

This Joe. Full of tender passion, taking what I gave with a sense of wonder and joy, and giving me double measure in return.

My friend. My daughter's hero. My heart.

"I love you," I whispered.

He paused, his hands now holding my face, thumbs tracing my cheekbones. "I thought it was too late, that I'd waited too long."

With one more dip of his chin, our lips mingled. *Please don't let this moment end...*

A squeal cut off my dreamy prayer. "Oh my goodness! Finally."

I felt Joe's smile as he broke our little dance, and couldn't help but chuckle. Turning my head to look at the bundle of energy to my left, I noted that Joe's head still rested against mine.

"What do you mean, finally?" My palms slid over Joe's gray sweater, and he pulled me into a hug.

Sydney twirled. "I mean *finally*. This was what I wanted for Christmas."

"Oh," I laughed. "I'm glad we could accommodate you."

With a grin she stepped closer, and Joe's hand fell away from my back to tuck her head against his leg. "So you're okay with me dating your mom?"

"Duh. It's about time you two figured out that you're in loooove."

I rolled my eyes. "Okay, smarty-pants. How about you say good night and go to bed."

A smirk slid over her face. "Good night." She spun on one foot and moved down the hall. Her faint sigh drifted back to our hearing. "It's better than a Disney movie."

Heat tickled my chest. The little princess.

When I looked back to Joe, his tender smile made my heart puddle. "See," he whispered, sneaking in another peck near my ear. "She's a wit. I told you you didn't need to worry."

Usually right, Joe White was. Sometimes that was annoying. But not that night. I snuggled against him, wrapping my arms around his waist, loving how he held me both securely and tenderly.

How had this happened? Could it be real?

"I thought you only loved Sydney." I pushed my head into his chest, overwhelmed by the wonder of it. "That you couldn't love me too."

"I can't even begin to tell you how wrong that is." He tipped my chin up and stroked the side of my face. Another brush of our mouths paused his words. "How much I love you, how much I want you both."

Favor. I'd prayed for favor in a good man's eyes, for me and for my daughter. God gave me so much more.

This ordinary life. It was really quite something.

Epilogue

The following Christmas...

With a tuck-and-roll maneuver, Joe ducked behind the snow drift we'd taken as our armory. With at least twenty snowballs waiting to be fired, we had a pretty decent shot at taking on the kid. If Sydney wouldn't cheat. The rascal.

"You need to tame your daughter. She's everywhere." Joe grabbed my waist from behind and nuzzled my neck.

"Uh, you're the one who got her out of those leg braces. I think this is your fault."

"How was I supposed to know she'd take off running like an Olympic champ?"

I leaned back against him and swiveled my neck to catch his mouth with mine. My stomach fluttered—but not just from his kisses, which still thrilled me. Instinctively, I flicked off my glove and palmed the spot on my lower abdomen.

Joe's eyes lit up, and his gloved hand covered mine, catching on the ring set that had marked a shift in our world. "Is it moving?"

"Yeah. Working out so it'll keep up with its big sister." I leaned into his embrace, inhaling contentment. "Syd's so excited. Almost more so than the fact that it'll be official in two months. She'll legally be Sydney White."

"How did I get that lucky?"

Biting my lip, I grinned. "Marrying me definitely helped."

His low laughter vibrated near my ear. "That was a highlight, for sure."

As I closed my eyes, scenes from last Christmas flashed through my memory. Sydney opening that Lego Palace and then throwing herself into Joe's arms. In her well-practiced Rapunzel voice, she proclaimed it was the "Best. Christmas. Ever."

When Joe slid a diamond ring over my finger later that night, I had to agree.

"I want us to be a family," he'd said.

I cried.

Guess he figured after five years of friendship, a week of official dating was more than adequate for a proposal. Who was I to argue?

When he asked Syd if he could marry me, and after the required year of waiting after our wedding, could he start the process of adoption, she wrapped her entire self around him like a baby monkey.

He took that as a yes. We were married two days before Valentine's Day.

Now our first Christmas together as a family was just three days away.

Resting against my husband—oh my word, that still sent chills over my arms—I let scenes from the past year flash through my memory. Our wedding, small, sweet, and wonderful. Tiny, silver-threaded snowflakes covered the dress I wore. Joe smiled, fingering one on the strap over my right arm.

"You're a fan now?"

"Snowflakes, yes." I winked. "Winter...is tolerable. Fan would be going too far."

He kissed my forehead. "Fair enough."

I leaned into him for a moment, and then together we turned to our pastor, waiting for us with an approving grin.

Definitely a highlight moment.

In the spring, we worked to create a garden in Joe's— no, our backyard. Syd and I spent our afternoons squatting next to the tilled dirt, the black soil lying naked and plain to the sky above, until one day a little green seedling emerged from the black ground. It was thrilling.

That summer, Joe would often stoke a small fire in the metal pit he had in the backyard. He and I would sit and watch the orange flame dance while Sydney chased fireflies or roasted a mallow. Precious, amazing everyday moments.

That fall we carved pumpkins. Joe helped Sydney count the seeds from one of the medium-sized gourds. Every last one. He was a man of incredible patience, and he showed Sydney the wonder of everyday life. Like the fact that there were 536 seeds in that one pumpkin. Pretty outstanding, right?

Leaning against Joe, tucked behind that drift and preparing for another snow-bomb attack, I shut my eyes and let wonder fall over me, grabbing hold of everything God had revealed over the past year.

He purposed my life. I could put my hand in His and

trust Him because He loved me. He saw me, and my life mattered to Him. And when I rested in that, I no longer felt completely ordinary and beyond His notice—I felt gratitude. Enormous, tear-beckoning gratefulness for His unmerited favor. And the voices of guilt drowned in that heart full of thanksgiving.

To think God opened my eyes to this amazing truth with a snowflake. And one exceptional man.

Truly, there are no ordinary snowflakes, because they are crafted by an extraordinary God.

~The End~

Many, O LORD my God, are Your wonderful works
Which You have done;
And Your thoughts toward us
Cannot be recounted to You in order;
If I would declare and speak of them,
They are more than can be numbered.

~Psalm 40:5 NKJV~

Dear Readers,

Thank you so much for taking this winter-wonderland trip with me. I loved writing this story. Kale, Joe, Sydney, and Craig were a much-needed break from the heavier stories I've written, but to be honest, they taught me every bit as much as the other characters from other books.

This one is for the moms. We worry. We compare. We get sucked into social media and printed articles that tell how to do what we do and seemingly all of the things we are doing or have done wrong. I know. I've got four kids of my own, and I can't tell you how many nights I've wasted, missing the sleep I desperately needed, worrying about the many ways I was messing up. They're my kids, my responsibility, right? How could God trust me with that?

Let's implant this in our hearts. He has given us all we need in Christ. All. We. Need. So, with Kale, let's grab hold of this:

Stop seeking badges of honor and begin prioritizing touches of grace.

God sees us. Sees our tired hearts, doing the best we know how. How much we love our kids and really want His best for them. And, sweet mom, you're doing fine. Grab His priorities and trust Him. He has granted you favor to do this job, and to do it well.

He's given you all you need.

From one relieved mommy's heart to another,

Jen

Other Books Available From Jen:

Reclaimed

The Carpenter's Daughter

Grace Revealed Series:
Blue Columbine
Red Rose Bouquet

Please visit Jen's website for more info, or just to chat.
She'd love to hear from you!

www.authorjenrodewald.com

https://www.facebook.com/authorjenrodewald

Made in the USA
Middletown, DE
26 November 2017